HOME SWEET MOTEL

More Favorites by
CHRIS GRABENSTEIN

Escape from Mr. Lemoncello's Library
Mr. Lemoncello's Library Olympics
Mr. Lemoncello's Great Library Race
The Island of Dr. Libris
Welcome to Wonderland: Beach Party Surf Monkey
Welcome to Wonderland: Sandapalooza Shake-Up

THE HAUNTED MYSTERY SERIES
The Crossroads
The Demons' Door
The Zombie Awakening
The Black Heart Crypt

COAUTHORED WITH JAMES PATTERSON
Daniel X: Armageddon
Daniel X: Lights Out
House of Robots
House of Robots: Robots Go Wild!
House of Robots: Robot Revolution
I Funny
I Even Funnier
I Totally Funniest
I Funny TV
I Funny: School of Laughs
Jacky Ha-Ha
Pottymouth and Stoopid
Treasure Hunters
Treasure Hunters: Danger Down the Nile
Treasure Hunters: Secret of the Forbidden City
Treasure Hunters: Peril at the Top of the World
Treasure Hunters: Quest for the City of Gold
Word of Mouse

HOME SWEET MOTEL

CHRIS GRABENSTEIN

illustrated by Brooklyn Allen

A Yearling Book

All rights reserved. Published in the United States by Yearling,
an imprint of Random House Children's Books, a division of
Penguin Random House LLC, New York. Originally
published in hardcover in the United States by
Random House Children's Books, New York, in 2016.

Yearling and the jumping horse design are registered
trademarks of Penguin Random House LLC.

Visit us on the Web! rhcbooks.com

Educators and librarians, for a variety of teaching tools,
visit us at RHTeachersLibrarians.com

The Library of Congress has cataloged the
hardcover edition of this work as follows:
Names: Grabenstein, Chris, author. | Allen, Brooke, illustrator.
Title: Welcome to wonderland: Home sweet motel / Chris Grabenstein ;
illustrated by Brooke Allen.
Description: First edition. | New York : Random House, [2016] |
Series: Welcome to Wonderland ; Book 1 | Summary: "P.T. and
his friend Gloria must solve a mystery at the world's wackiest
motel: The Wonderland" —Provided by publisher.
Identifiers: LCCN 2015030808 | ISBN 978-0-553-53602-7 (hardcover) |
ISBN 978-0-553-53603-4 (hardcover library binding) |
ISBN 978-0-553-53604-1 (ebook)
Subjects: | CYAC: Mystery and detective stories. |
Hotels, motels, etc.—Fiction.
Classification: LCC PZ7.G7487 Ho 2016 | DDC [Fic]—dc23

ISBN 978-0-553-53605-8 (pbk.)

Printed in the United States of America
10 9 8 7 6 5 4 3 2
First Yearling Edition 2018

For my mom
and my memories of
Treasure Island, Florida
—CG

Gator Tales

Like I told my friends at school, living in a motel is always exciting—especially during an alligator attack.

"To this day, nobody knows how that giant alligator made it up to the second-floor balcony of my family's motel on St. Pete Beach," I told my audience.

The cafeteria was so quiet you could've heard a taco shell snap.

"Maybe it took the steps. Maybe it just stood up, locked its teeth on a porch railing, and flipped itself up and over in a mighty somersault swoop. The thing was strong, people. Very, very strong.

"I heard Clara, my favorite housekeeper, scream, '¡Monstruo, Señor Wilkie! ¡Monstruo!'

"'Run!' I shouted, because Clara's always been like a second mom to me and I wanted her to be alive enough to see her daughter graduate from med school.

"Well, she didn't need me to shout it twice. Clara abandoned her laundry cart while that alligator raced toward the room at the far end of the balcony. And I knew why: the chicken.

"See, the family in room 233—a mom, a dad, two kids, and a baby—had just gone upstairs with a whole bucket of the stuff. Heck, I could smell it twenty doors down. The giant alligator? He smelled that secret blend of eleven herbs and spices all the way back at his little lake on the Bayside Golf Course, where, legend has it, he's chomped off a few ball divers' arms.

"Thinking fast and running faster, I made it to Clara's deserted laundry cart. I grabbed a few rolls of toilet paper and lobbed them like hand grenades. The T.P. conked the gator on his head just as he was about to chomp through the terrified family's door.

"That's when the giant lizard whipped around.

He looked at me with those big bowling-ball eyes. Forget the chicken. He wanted *me*! He roared like smelly thunder and sprinted down the balcony.

"I just grinned. Because the gator was doing exactly what I wanted him to do. While he barreled ahead on stubby legs, I braced my feet on the bumper of the laundry cart. I lashed several towels together to create a long terry-cloth lasso. I twirled it over my head. I waited for my moment.

"When the gator was five, maybe six, feet away, I flung out my towel rope, aiming for his wide-open mouth. He clamped down. I tugged back. My lasso locked on a jagged tooth. 'Hee-yah!' I shouted. 'Giddyup!' The monster took off.

"What happened next, you wonder? Well, I rode that laundry cart all the way back to the crazy alligator's golf course, where I sent the gator scurrying down into its water hazard. 'And stay away from our motel,' I hollered, and I guess that gator listened, because he's never dared return."

When I finished, everyone applauded, even Ms. Nagler, the teacher on cafeteria duty. She raised her hand to ask a question.

"Yes, ma'am?"

"How'd you and the alligator get down from the second floor?"

I winked. "One step at a time, Ms. Nagler. One step at a time."

She, and everybody else, laughed.

Yep, everybody at Ponce de León Middle School loves a good P. T. Wilkie story.

Except, of course, Mr. Frumpkes.

He came into the cafeteria just in time to hear my big finish.

And like always, he wasn't smiling.

Truth and Consequences

"**M**r. Wilkie?" Mr. Frumpkes had his hands on his hips and his eyes on me. "Lunch is over."

Right on cue, the bell signaling the end of lunch period started clanging.

Fact: Alligators cannot run fast for long distances. They are cold-blooded and therefore quickly deplete their energy reserves. The alligator in your story could NOT have transported you to a golf course two miles away.

Between you and me, I sometimes think Mr. Frumpkes has telepathic powers. He can make the class-change bell ring just by thinking about it.

"Ah," he said, clearly enjoying the earsplitting rattle and clanks. "Now we don't have to listen to any more of Mr. Wilkie's outrageously ridiculous tales!"

My first class right after lunch?

History with Mr. Frumpkes, of course.

He paced back and forth at the front of the room with his hands clasped behind his back.

"Facts are important, boys and girls," he said. "They lead us to the truth. Here at the Ponce de León Middle School, we have a motto: *'Vincit omnia veritas!'*"

I couldn't resist making a wisecrack. "I thought our school motto was 'Go, Conquistadors!'"

Mr. Frumpkes stopped pacing so he could glare at me some more.

"*'Vincit omnia veritas'* is Latin, Mr. Wilkie. It means 'The truth conquers all.'"

"So it *is* like 'Go, Conquistadors!' because conquistadors conquered stuff and—"

"I'm beginning to understand why your father never shows up at parent-teacher conferences, Mr. Wilkie."

Okay. That hurt. My ears were burning.

"But since Mr. Wilkie seems fixated on conquistadors," said Mr. Frumpkes, "here is everybody's brand-new homework assignment."

"Awww," groaned the whole classroom.

"Don't groan at me. Groan at your immature classmate! Thanks to Mr. Wilkie, you are all required to write a one-thousand-word essay filled with cold, hard facts about the man whom this middle school is named after: the famous Spanish conquistador Ponce de León. Your papers are due on Monday."

"Whoa," said my friend Pinky Nelligan. "Monday is the start of Spring Break."

"Fine," said Mr. Frumpkes. "Your papers are due tomorrow. Friday."

More groans.

"Let this be a lesson to you all: facts are more important than fiction."

I was about to disagree and tell Mr. Frumpkes that I think some stories have more power than all the facts you can find on Google.

But I didn't.

Because *everybody* in the classroom was making stink faces at me.

I Scream, You Scream

I refused to let Mr. Frumpkes win.

"Oh, before I forget—quick announcement: you guys are all invited to the Wonderland Motel after school today. My grandpa wants to try out his new outdoor ice-cream dispenser. The ice cream is free, limit one per guest."

The groans and moans of my classmates turned into whoops of joy. Mr. Frumpkes tried to restore order by banging on his desk with a tape dispenser.

"We're here to discuss history, Mr. Wilkie! Not free ice cream!"

But everybody loves free ice cream.

That's just a cold, hard fact.

Unless it's soft-serve.

Then it's kind of custardy.

Welcome to Wonderland

The Wonderland, the motel my family owns and operates on St. Pete Beach, used to be called Walt Wilkie's Wonder World.

It was a resort and small-time amusement park my grandfather opened back in October 1970—exactly one year before that other Walt opened Disney World over in Orlando.

"We had a very good year, P.T.," Grandpa always tells me. "A very good year."

Now the Wonderland is just a motel with a lot of wacky decorations and tons of incredible stories but not too many paying customers.

There's even a sausage-and-cheese-loving mouse out back named Morty D. Mouse. Grandpa was going to call him Mikey Mouse, but, well, like I said, Disney World opened.

My mom is the motel manager. I think that's why she frowns a lot and nibbles so many pencils. The Wonderland can "barely make ends meet," she tells me. Constantly. That means we'll never be rich hotel tycoons like the Hiltons, I guess.

Mom and I live in room 101/102, right behind the front desk. The lobby is our living room (complete with two soda machines, a snack pantry, and tons of brochures).

Grandpa lives in a one-bedroom apartment over the maintenance shed near the swimming pool.

He likes to tinker with his "attractions" back there. Right now, he is trying to fix up a smiling goober he bought from a "Hot Boiled Peanuts" stand in Georgia. He thinks with enough green, orange, and yellow paint, he can turn Mr. Peanut into some sort of smiling tropical fruit—like that's all the Wonderland needs to make it *Florida Fun in the Sun* magazine's "Hottest Family Attraction in the Sunshine State" (a title Grandpa really wants to snatch away from Disney World someday).

One thing's for sure: the Wonderland Motel is the best place a kid could ever live.

There's daily maid service. My toilet is sanitized for my protection.

I feel so much safer. Now it can't bite me in the butt.

sanitized for your protection

We have more ice than Antarctica, plus free cable and HBO. Also, if you know how to bump the glass just right, you can score *two* bags of chips every time you buy one from the vending machine.

And now Grandpa's set up a soft-serve ice-cream dispenser poolside?

Yep. The Wonderland is kid heaven. There's always something wild 'n' wacky going on—which is just the way I like it.

Amenities

"**W**e can't afford to give away free ice cream, Dad," Mom told Grandpa when she saw me and my friends swirling our cones under the pump handle.

Pinky Nelligan wasn't using a cone. He just stuck his face under the nozzle.

I mouthed the words "We can barely make ends meet" before Mom said it out loud—for the ten billionth time.

"Relax, Wanda," said Grandpa. "This is a resort. We need the little extras, what they call amenities, to attract customers."

"These aren't customers," said Mom. "These are P.T.'s friends from school."

"Ah," said Grandpa, raising his finger the way he does when he's about to say something super important, "but one day they'll grow up and have

families of their own and they'll say, 'Remember that wonderful resort in Florida with the all-you-can-eat ice-cream buffet poolside? That was such a lovely amenity. Let's go there on our next vacation!'"

He slurped his can of Dr. Brown's Cel-Ray soda to punctuate his point. By the way—Cel-Ray soda? Yep. It's celery-flavored. Don't ask.

Mom sighed. "Dad?"

"Yes, Wanda?"

"These kids all live in Florida. They're not coming here for vacation when they grow up."

"What if they move to Maine? Maybe Canada?"

"I think my friend Julie Scarboro likes Canada," I said, trying to help Grandpa out. "I know she likes maple syrup. And Kip Rand over there knows somebody who lives in Maine."

"He's my cousin," said the Kipster helpfully. "He loves lobster."

"Can we have, like, seconds?" asked Porter Malkiel, another friend from school, who'd never been to Canada and didn't know anybody in Maine but could definitely scarf down ice-cream cones.

"Help yourself, Porter," said Grandpa. "It's an amenity."

Mom sighed again and walked away, mumbling what she always mumbled when she sighed twice and walked away: "Why do I have to be the only grown-up in this family?"

I don't know who she was asking.

Or if she ever got an answer.

I was too busy enjoying all that free ice cream with my friends.

Spring Broken

Believe it or not, while we were hanging out, scarfing down gallons of free ice cream, Pinky Nelligan started complaining about Spring Break, the way he likes to complain about everything.

It's sort of how he earned his nickname. Sometimes when he's moaning and groaning about stuff, his face turns pink. Like boiled shrimp.

"Kids all over America come to Florida for Spring Break. Where are *we* supposed to go?"

"You guys are always welcome here," I told him.

"No disrespect, P.T.," said Julie Scarboro, "but after you play one hundred rounds of your grandfather's Pirate Pete's Putt-Putt course, it sort of loses its thrill."

"All Spring Break means for us," whined Pinky, "is longer lines at McDonald's, longer lines at the movie theater, and longer lines at every stoplight between McDonald's and the movie theater."

"Spring Break also means no school," I said, because as you'll see, I like to look on the bright side, even when it's darker than the inside of my pants pockets at midnight.

Not that I've ever actually looked inside my pants pockets that late at night, but you get the idea. I'm an optimist. It's hard not to be when you live in a place where a giant peanut can magically become a Hawaiian Happy-Stinky Fruit with a face.

"Besides," I said, "Spring Break means no Mr. Frumpkes for a whole week."

"Speaking of Mr. Grumpface," said Julie, checking the time on her smartphone, "I'd better head home. Time to work on my Ponce de León essay . . ."

And that's when the new kid, Brendan Sullivan Barrett, piped up.

Houston, We Have a Problem

"Is it true what Mr. Frumpkes said?" Brendan asked with a twang. He and his family had just moved to Florida from Texas. "Your dad doesn't ever go to parent-teacher conferences?"

"Nope," I said. "He can't."

"Why not?"

I pointed to the rocket ship perched on the other side of the pool fence.

"NASA won't let him," I explained.

"You mean the space people? Like we had in Houston?"

"That's right. NASA's here in Florida, too. Over at Cape Canaveral. My dad is what they call an undercover astronaut."

"Huh," said Julie. "I thought you told us he was on the road with the Ringling Brothers and Barnum and Bailey circus."

"That's his cover story," I said. "NASA cooked it up to explain why he hasn't been home for so long. But between you and me, Brendan, there's a reason my grandfather erected that rocket ship twelve years ago, on the day I was born. It's to remind us all that my dad volunteered for a mission that no other astronaut was brave enough to undertake—a mission that will, one day, benefit you and me and all of humanity."

"You're making this up," said Brendan.

"No, Brendan. Sometimes I wish I were. Do you know how long it takes our fastest spaceship to reach Nigel Fifteen?"

"Nigel Fifteen? Who's he?"

"It's not a he," I said.

"It's a planet in a nearby solar system," said Pinky, who'd heard me tell this story before. "Right in the Goldilocks Zone!"

I nodded. "What Pinky means is that Nigel

Fifteen is an Earth-type planet orbiting its star at a distance that makes it not too hot, not too cold. It's just right for human life. Unfortunately, it takes eleven years to fly there, even if you use the gravitational pull of Jupiter to slingshot your supersecret high-speed spacecraft out of our solar system."

"Wow," said Brendan.

"NASA figures Dad will land sometime next year. Probably right around Christmas. If Nigel Fifteen lives up to its promise, then those of us in middle school right now might be the first colonists to live on that distant planet in twenty or thirty years."

"So we could be like Ponce de León," said Brendan, sounding excited. "Only instead of exploring Florida, we could go explore Nigel Fifteen!"

"Ponce de León," groaned Julie. "Essay. Yuck."

"Gotta go," said Pinky. "School's always trying to ruin my life."

"Yeah," said everybody else.

"Thanks for the ice cream," said Brendan. "And tonight when all the stars come out, guess what I'm going to do, P.T."

"Make a wish?"

"Nope. I'm gonna wave at your dad!"

By five o'clock, everybody was gone—leaving me alone with a gurgling ice-cream machine, a trickling waterslide, Grandpa's fiberglass rocket ship, and a made-up story that was starting to seem a lot more real than my dad ever had.

Pouncing on Ponce

The next day, we were all right back in history class with Mr. Frumpkes.

"Who would like to be the first to give his or her oral report on Ponce de León?" he asked with manic glee.

"Oral report?" said Julie. "You just said we had to write an essay."

"I changed my mind. Teacher's prerogative. We reserve the right to change our minds whenever the mood strikes."

All of us (including me) slumped down in our seats with our eyes glued to the tops of our desks.

"Fine," said Mr. Frumpkes. "I'll choose for you."

He did this annoying thing he does sometimes, where he closes his eyes and swirls his finger around and around over his grade book.

"Helicopter, helicopter, who gets to go?"

After about three more rotations, he jabbed his finger down on the page and read the name it landed on.

"Peter Paul Nelligan?"

Pinky.

"I knew he'd call on me," Pinky grumbled as he rose beside his desk. He cleared his throat. Ruffled his paper. The tips of his ears turned pink.

"Juan Ponce de León had a very unusual name," he read from his essay. "You don't meet many guys named Juan Ponce these days. I wonder if his parents named him that because he only had one pair of pants. You know, One Pants/Juan Ponce . . ."

"Mr. Nelligan?" said Mr. Frumpkes. "Did you even write an essay?"

"Yes, sir." Pinky showed the teacher his paper. The lines were filled with blue ink. "I guess I was kind of hung up on his name."

"And I guess I'm going to have to give you an F."

Mr. Frumpkes had his pen poised over his grade book.

"An F?" I said, standing up. "Pinky—I mean, Peter Paul—is just a little nervous, sir. Heck, I would be, too, if I had to go first."

"Are you volunteering to read your essay, Mr. Wilkie?"

"Sure. Right after I read Pinky's so you can

hear how good it is and why he deserves an A, not an F."

I reached out my hand. Pinky gave me his paper.

"Thanks, man," he mumbled.

I shot him a wink. "I've got this," I whispered back.

It was time for another triumph of fiction over fact. After all, I was the one who'd gotten us into this essay-writing mess. Voice booming, I pretended to read the report Pinky had written, but mostly I was improvising, making junk up.

"Young Juan Ponce de León, the boy with the funny first name, dreamed of becoming *El Conquistador Valiente*. And so, one day—or 'Juan day'—he put on his one pair of puffy pants, his feathered helmet, and his armor and set sail with Christopher Columbus. Yes, it is a little-known fact that Juan Ponce de León, who was born in Spain in 1460, began his career as an explorer as part of Columbus's second expedition to the New World in 1493."

Okay. I had done my homework. Our motel also has free Wi-Fi. I just hoped I could pretend to read Pinky's paper long enough that I wouldn't have to read any of my own, because basically it had all the same stuff in it.

"Ponce de León gave Florida its name because, much like a florist's shop, it was a 'place of flowers.'"

"That's not true," said Mr. Frumpkes.

"Oh, but it is, Mr. Frumpkes," I said with a smile. "'*La Florida*' means 'the flowery land.' Probably because Ponce de León first spotted our fair peninsula on April 2, 1513, during the flowery Easter season, which is known in Spanish as *Pascua Florida*. If he had arrived closer to Christmas, we might all be living in the state of Feliznavida."

"Huh," grunted Mr. Frumpkes. "I did not know that."

I could've gloated, but I just kept going.

"However, what Ponce de León was really looking for when he hiked around our peninsula was the legendary—dare I say *mythical*—Fountain of Youth. Sure, he was searching for gold and, on his day off, he discovered Puerto Rico, but he really wanted to locate the magical spring he'd heard so many stories about. The locals told him it gushed water that could make old people turn young again. Alas, judging from my grandfather and certain other, shall we say, *elderly* individuals . . ."

I took a pause so everybody could check out Mr. Frumpkes's comb-over—six greasy strands of hair that couldn't hide his chrome dome.

". . . the great conquistador never found his fountain. He did discover Cape Canaveral and the Dry Tortugas, but no fountain. Especially not on the Dry Tortugas, because they were dry and shaped like turtles, which can live to be some of the oldest, most non-youthful creatures on earth . . ."

I went on like that for nearly twenty minutes.

By the time I was done, I had recited every fact and figure there was to report on Señor Juan Ponce de León. Nobody else had to stand up and give an oral report.

The bell rang and we were all free of Mr. Frumpkes for a whole week.

I hurried home to the Wonderland feeling great—until I saw Mom behind the front desk, talking to a man in a dark suit.

I knew he wasn't there to pick up a SeaWorld brochure or play Pirate Pete's Putt-Putt course.

All the News I Can't Use

Nobody wears dark suits in Florida unless they're going to a funeral or have something super serious to discuss.

This guy seemed like he thought his shiny midnight-blue outfit made him look slick. He kept tugging his tie and flicking his bangs while checking out his reflection in our glossy (but fake) marble countertop.

"P.T., mind the front desk," said Mom, dialing down the volume knob on the walkie-talkie she wore clipped to her belt. "I need to talk to Mr. Pompano in my office."

"It's Pom-*PAN*-o," said the man in the suit.

"Sorry," said Mom.

The guy just nodded like she should be.

"P.T.?" said Mom.

"Okay," I said with a shrug.

"This way, Mr., uh, Pom-*PAN*-o . . ."

She held open the door to her tiny office and quickly whispered, "Keep Grandpa busy!"

"What? Why?"

"Mr. Pompano is from *the bank*."

Oh-kay. Now I understood.

Grandpa isn't very good at grown-up stuff like banking or staying awake while driving. He's better at turning smiling peanut heads into exotic Hawaiian fruits. Or burping up gross salad gas after guzzling Cel-Ray soda. Or telling stories about how things used to be "back in the day."

While I guarded the lobby, a dad and a daughter came in. I didn't recognize either one of them. They had to be that very rarest of rare tropical birds: paying customers.

"Hi there," said the dad. "I'm Manuel 'Manny' Ortega, new to the sports team at WTSP—Tampa Bay, St. Petersburg, and Sarasota's channel ten. We've got the news you need when you need it. Unless you need it right now, because I'm not on the air until five. Catch me right after Dr. Phil."

"You do sports, Dad," said his daughter, rolling her eyes. She looked about the same age as me. "Not news."

"Sports *is* news. We always step up to the plate. And remember: there is no 'I' in 'team.'"

I was just sort of nodding. Mr. Ortega, who sounded like a smooth radio deejay, talked very, very fast.

"We just checked in," said his daughter. "I'm Gloria. My dad lost our room key."

"Fumbled it behind my own goal line," said her dad.

"He dropped it in the swimming pool."

"Kudos on that underwater pool-cleaning robot," said Mr. Ortega. "It gave one hundred and ten percent."

"That's mathematically impossible, Dad."

"Be that as it may, the robot showed us everything it had out there today. Ate the key in ten seconds flat. A new outdoor pool record!"

"Do we get CNBC on our cable?" asked Gloria.

"I think so. Is that the one with the *Today* show?"

"Whoa there, kiddo," said her father with another blindingly bright smile. "In our family, we only watch the CBS morning news on WTSP—CBS channel ten."

"Right," said Gloria. "This week that's what we watch. Next week? Who knows what channel you'll be on." She turned to me. "CNBC is a business news channel. You know, stock markets, financial data, earnings reports."

"That's the one with all the numbers and junk, right?"

Now Gloria rolled her eyes at me instead of her dad.

"Riiiight," she said. "The numbers and junk."

"I think it's, like, channel forty-six. I've skipped over it a few times on my way to HBO or ESPN."

"Oooh," said Mr. Ortega. "ESPN. The top dogs. The big kahunas. Gotta keep my eyes on that prize. It's fourth and long, and I'm going for six!"

I pulled open the drawer where we keep the spare room keys. We don't do those magnetic cards you swipe through a reader. Grandpa prefers the old-fashioned kind with a big plastic fob, a tag that says, "Drop in any mailbox. We guarantee postage!" It does not say, "Drop in the nearest swimming pool."

"So what room are you guys in?" I asked.

"Second floor," said Gloria. "Room 233."

I shot her one of my slyest winks. "You didn't sneak a bucket of chicken up there, did you?"

"Huh?"

"Never mind. Long story."

I might've told her about the alligator and the laundry cart and how I rode it chariot-style to a nearby golf course. I might've even added a few new details, like what happened at the water hazard when I discovered it was infested with sharks.

But I didn't have time.

I could see Grandpa ambling across the parking lot.

He was making a beeline for the front office.

Listen up, sharks. Tomorrow I'm taking all of you guys to the Jaws exhibit at Universal Studios!

Happy-Stinky Fruit

"Here you go," I said, tossing Gloria Ortega a spare key to room 233.

I hopped over the check-in counter and bopped the desk bell to alert Mom that I'd just spotted Grandpa.

"Now, if you two don't mind," I said, ushering the Ortegas toward the door, "we need to lock up the lobby so our staff can restock the Coke machine."

"Seriously?" said Gloria.

"Oh, yeah. There's a lot of coin counting involved. Have to roll the pennies in those little paper sleeves . . ."

"The Coke machine takes pennies?"

"It's an old machine."

Gloria shook her head. Mr. Ortega gave me a jaunty salute.

"Play like a champion today," he said.

"Yes, sir." I escorted them both out of the lobby and locked the door.

While the Ortegas climbed the steps to the second floor, I headed across the parking lot to intercept Grandpa.

"Hey, Grandpa, what's up?"

"Hmmm?"

He had that far-off look in his eye, the one he always gets when he's dreaming up a new "attraction."

"Wanda?" he said into his walkie-talkie. "Pick up. I have a huge idea! This is bigger than those mer-kids we did in the swimming pool with the windup baby dolls. Wanda? Where are you?"

"Bigger than the mer-kids?" I said. "The mer-kids were huge. What is it, Grandpa?"

He burped. Once again, the scent of celery filled the air.

"P.T., I just figured out the ideal, perfect location for our new Happy-Stinky Fruit! We should put it in the lobby with the cat's litter box hidden inside so when people check in, the Happy-Stinky Fruit would actually *stink*! It'd be incredible. Disney doesn't have anything like it. None of their attractions stink. We're finally going to show the world who's the top Walt in Florida. Me!"

"Neat idea, Grandpa. But I've got an even better one! I think the Happy-Stinky Fruit should go out back."

"Really? Where?"

"Come on. I'll show you."

I took Grandpa by the hand and led him to the rear parking lot, where you can still see a stretch of the narrow railroad tracks for the old ride-on train sunk into the asphalt.

It was about as far from the front office as we could go and still be on Wonderland property.

And that's exactly where Mom needed Grandpa.

Far, far away.

The Good Old Days

"**Y**ou see that pavilion?" I said. "We're not using it for anything except picnic tables. What if you put the sculpture inside and we called it the Hawaiian Picnic Island?"

Grandpa was shaking his head.

"Nope, nope, nope," he said as we walked over to it. "Can't do that, P.T. This is the Wonder World Express Depot."

"It is?" I said, pretending I didn't know what the ramshackle shed used to be.

"Back in the day, this is where we'd load up the railroad cars."

"Is this where you met the lady with the scarf?" I asked, knowing Grandpa would launch into his favorite story—the one about the beautiful blonde in the sunglasses and red polka-dot scarf. I'd listen. It would give Mom enough time to finish with the banker.

Grandpa sat down at one of the picnic tables and patted the bench for me to join him.

"This is the exact spot," said Grandpa. He had a different kind of dreamy look in his eyes. "Of course, this was way back—before you were born. Before your mother was born. It was even before I met your grandmother, may she rest in peace. The year was 1973. Disney World was already open, so most of the glamorous movie stars and Hollywood types were skipping St. Pete and heading over to Orlando. But not my blonde."

"Was she a movie star?"

"If she wasn't, she should've been. Oh, she was beautiful, P.T. *Beautiful.*

"She was here for a whole week. Sheila was her name. She must've taken a half dozen train rides around the property—one on every day of her stay. She'd say, 'This place is perfect,' and I'd say, 'That's why we call it Wonder World, ma'am. It is full of marvels to behold and stories to be told!' My beautiful blond visitor wanted to know everything about every single display. The Mars rocket. Morty D. Mouse. Dino the Dinosaur. She was the first person I ever met who seemed to love Wonder World even more than I did."

"I love it, too, Grandpa," I said, because I knew he needed to hear somebody say it. Plus, I do love the Wonderland, the motel that Walt Wilkie's Wonder World turned into.

"On her last Saturday, after we took our train ride together, she told me she was hungry. Wanted pancakes. That made me smile. I thought I was the only one who liked a short stack of strawberry-banana pancakes for dinner. She headed down the boulevard to the IHOP. I never saw her again."

Grandpa sniffled a little. I think he might've been tearing up.

"I don't know why she never came back," Grandpa said with a sigh. "But I will never, *ever* forget her face. Like an angel, she was. An angel with a red polka-dot scarf instead of a halo."

I nodded.

We sat and didn't say anything.

After a few minutes, I asked him, "You ever think about running the railroad again? Putting the train back on the tracks?"

"Sometimes. But it would take a lot of work, P.T. A *lot* of work." He stood up and started wandering off. "First I'd need to overhaul the engine, repaint the cars and the caboose, find my engineer's cap. . . ."

He was in that dreamy zone again, heading back to his workshop behind the swimming pool to tinker with his oversized toy train.

I bolted to the lobby to unlock the front door.

I didn't need to.

The man in the dark suit was already seated in his purring convertible. Mom was trying to talk to him over the engine noise.

"We need more than a month, Mr. Pompano," I heard her say.

"It's Pom-*PAN*-o," shouted the banker, checking his reflection, once again, in the rearview mirror. "And you and your motel are standing in the way of progress, Ms. Wilkie. This property could be huge. I mean colossal. Hey, if you have to think, why not think big? Enjoy the rest of your day."

He sped out of the parking lot.

Mom didn't look very happy.

In fact, if I didn't know her better, I'd say she looked like she might cry.

The Bad New Days

But I'd be wrong.

My mother, Ms. Wanda Wilkie, never cries.

That queasy look I saw on her face?

That was just anger. Mom was mad.

"How dare he," she muttered, storming back into the lobby. She was talking to herself, not me. "One month? How can anybody scrape together one hundred thousand dollars in one month?"

She banged the Coke machine in the sweet spot between the Sprite and Fanta buttons. A frosty bottle of diet cola clunked down into the pickup bin.

Mom started feeding quarters into the machine's money slot anyway.

"No more freebies, P.T."

"Okay."

As her coins plunked, one by one, into the

machine, she said, "Now we only have to come up with ninety-nine thousand nine hundred and ninety-nine dollars."

"Why does that man want all that money?"

"Because we owe it to him. Five years ago, Grandpa took out a one-hundred-thousand-dollar loan with a balloon payment. Of course, he never told *me* about it."

"You have to pay with balloons?"

"P.T.?"

Mom gave me the double raised eyebrows. That always means my cute remarks are not currently considered to be all that cute.

"Okay," I said, "so what does a balloon payment really mean?"

"It means that at a certain point in time—let's say thirty days from today—the entire loan has to be paid back in full."

"But what if we can't pay it back?"

"The bank takes over the motel."

"You mean that guy in the suit will be working behind the front desk?"

"No, P.T. If we can't pay off our debt, the bank will sell the Wonderland to somebody else. Probably somebody with 'huge' and 'colossal' plans, like tearing it down so they can put in condos and a strip mall. But I'm not going to let that happen."

Mom stomped into the office, probably to try to

come up with a way to save the only home I've ever known. I never dreamed somebody would want to tear it down and build something ordinary and boring.

Come on. This is the Wonderland.

There's nothing ordinary or boring about it!

At least there won't be as long as my family owns it.

Story Time

Now, if this were one of my stories, this is when Grandpa's glamorous friend in the red polka-dot scarf would dramatically return to the Wonderland.

Turns out, she really *is* a movie star, just like Grandpa suspected, and she has come back to Florida to film *Alligator Allie Six,* the fifth sequel in her blockbuster superhero series. She insists that movie scenes need to be filmed at our motel and that the movie people pay us at least one million dollars.

"I want a train chase," she tells her producers. "With tiny trains."

So the movie people give us all the money we need to pay off the balloon loan, and Grandpa gets to rebuild his railroad. Only, this time, the Wonderland

Express is a levitating bullet train that floats above the rails as it whooshes along at supersonic speeds.

The action scenes from the new movie are awesome.

Alligator Allie turns into the masked avenger known as Gator Girl. With her steel-trap, razor-sharp jaws of death, she goes up against the arch-villain Banker Boy, who destroys people's lives by flinging paperwork at them like ninja stars. He also likes to bop people on the head with lead balloons.

"Beware of paper cuts, Gator Girl!" Banker Boy giggles maniacally, because that's just the way super villains roll.

"Thanks for the heads-up, pencil pusher," replies Gator Girl. "But it looks like you've been sitting behind a desk a little too long. You've really given me something to sink my teeth into—your ginormous butt!"

Yeah. That would be awesome.

Cold, hard fact: not gonna happen.

No Hollywood superhero is going to swoop in and save the day. No movie people are going to show up with a one-million-dollar check made out to the Wonderland Motel.

Maybe that's why I like stories so much more than facts. Facts are for bankers and Mr. Frumpkes. They usually don't do me, or my family, much good.

While Mom flipped through her ledgers and clacked computer keys, looking for a way out of the motel's financial mess, I went into my room to watch TV.

I passed over that CNBC channel with all the numbers crowding the screen and paused on an old black-and-white movie starring Mickey Rooney and Judy Garland. It was called *Babes in Arms*. The kids in it save their families from financial ruin by putting on a show in a barn.

Too bad the Wonderland doesn't have a barn.

Chatting with Cheeseball

Cheeseball, our cat, jumped into my lap.

"Guess what, Cheeseball. Grandpa wants to move your litter box out into the lobby so *everybody* can smell why we named you after a chunk of stinky cheese."

She purred like a motorboat and kneaded my stomach with her paws.

I think she wanted me to change the channel.

Cheeseball wasn't big on movies with major musical numbers and people singing at each other. They were way too loud.

I thumbed the remote and stopped on a true crime show. It was one of those *Unsolved Mysteries* stories. Apparently, back in 1973, two brothers, Sidney and Stanley Sneemer, cracked open

a swanky Miami hotel's safe and stole five million dollars' worth of diamonds and jewelry.

A few days after the burglary, the cops, following up on an anonymous phone tip, arrested Stanley Sneemer in Miami. Stanley didn't want to go to jail without his little brother, so he told the police where they could find Sidney. Both brothers were sentenced to long jail terms (they were still behind bars—in separate prisons), but the police never recovered any of the stolen jewels.

"Although the jewel thieves went to prison, where they remain to this day," boomed the TV announcer, *"the Miami Palm Tree Hotel heist remains . . . an Unsolved Mystery!"*

The last three words were said in some kind of weird echo chamber. The effect was so loud and spooky that Cheeseball leapt out of my lap.

I clicked off the TV.

"I wish I had a big brother," I said to Cheeseball, who was hiding under my bed. "The two of us could steal one hundred thousand dollars' worth of jewelry and give it to Mom. Not that Mom likes jewelry . . ."

Cheeseball crawled out just far enough to look up at me disapprovingly.

"Okay. You're right. Stealing's wrong. I wouldn't actually do it. But somebody's got to do something. We could lose the motel. Do you know what that means? No more amenities. No more maid service, free HBO, or Morty D. Mouse. No more ice cream poolside. No more pool!"

Cheeseball meowed. I might've been scaring her.

"Relax," I said. "We'll be okay. I don't know how, but Mom'll figure something out. She always does."

I just hoped she had one more miracle left.

Greetings from Texas

"Who knows?" I said to Cheeseball, who'd hopped back into my lap. "Maybe my dad will actually show up sometime in the next thirty days and save us."

Cheeseball started purring again.

"Maybe he's some kind of Texas oil baron. This new kid at school, Brendan, told me about all the billionaire oil barons they have in Texas. That's probably why my father had to leave Florida. One of his oil wells hit a gusher, and he had to go man the pumps before it spewed black gold and Texas tea all over his next-door neighbor's front lawn. But if you ask me, my dad made a *huge* mistake not staying here with Mom and me. Sure, he probably eats barbecued ribs and brisket on a daily basis, but face it, Cheeseball: even a Dallas mansion isn't as awesome as a beachfront motel."

Cheeseball rolled over so I could scratch her tummy.

"Mansions might have swimming pools, but they don't have gigantic ice machines or ice buckets lined with plastic bags. They definitely don't have giant fiberglass statues of dinosaurs."

Yep, my father had definitely made a bad move when he left the Wonderland.

I just hoped Mom, Grandpa, and I wouldn't have to leave our motel home, too.

Spring Break's Over Already?

The next morning, Saturday, Mom woke me up at seven o'clock with even worse news.

"I need you to help around the motel, P.T.," she said while I was still rubbing the sleep gunk out of my eyes. "Since next week is Spring Break, you can work here."

"Work? What exactly do you mean when you say the word 'work'?"

"Well, for starters, you can pick up your towels and make your own bed."

"And what are the housekeepers going to do?"

"I had to let two of them go."

"What? How come?"

"To save money. And no more free sodas or snacks from the vending machines."

Wow. This was way worse than I'd thought it would be.

"What about ice?" I asked. "Is that still free?"

"There is no such thing as free ice, P.T. We have to pay for the water and the electricity and the plastic liners for the ice buckets and . . ."

Youch.

If this kept up, we might as well let the bank take the motel and move into a house. Then again, I wasn't exactly sure how we'd be able to afford a house if Mom didn't have any money. Unless, of course, we could trade our one motel for four little green houses, like in Monopoly.

Fact: life doesn't usually have the same rules as a board game.

And if we couldn't pay off the banker, we might lose more than just a turn.

Sour Grapefruits

Mom and I went into our little kitchenette.

I noticed that she hadn't brought in our usual two doughnuts from the free breakfast buffet: a chocolate frosted with sprinkles for me, a powdered cinnamon for her.

Instead, I saw two half grapefruits sitting in bowls. I was pretty sure they'd come from the grapefruit tree out back in the middle of Grandpa's Putt-Putt golf course.

For lunch, we'd probably have to eat the insides of the coconuts Grandpa scoops clean to make pirate-head souvenirs for the gift shop. Did you know you can ship a Welcome to Wonderland coconut to anyone anywhere in America just by slapping an address label and some

stamps on its hairy husk? You don't need a box or anything; you just mail the coconut. It's a fact. You can look it up.

Of course, not too many people wanted to mail souvenir coconuts from the Wonderland Motel to their friends. If more did, maybe we wouldn't have owed the bank one hundred thousand dollars.

"It's the first week of Spring Break and only *half* of our rooms are booked," said Mom.

I sank my serrated spoon into the edge of the pinkish fruit wedge—and accidentally squirted Mom in the eye.

She didn't even flinch.

She was too focused on motel money matters.

"We need to keep trimming the budget," she said, mostly to herself. "Maybe auction off some of your grandfather's knickknacks to collectors."

"Knickknacks?"

"The rocket ship. The jackalope. Morty D. Mouse. That giant smiling peanut he bought in Georgia."

"It's a Hawaiian Happy-Stinky Fruit now," I told her.

"Fine. Maybe somebody in Hawaii will bid on it. I'll take a picture and post it on eBay this afternoon."

"But Grandpa loves all that stuff."

"So do I. But we have to do what we have to do."

She locked eyes with me.

I had a feeling I was about to find out what else I had to do that had to be done.

"I need you to clean the pool today, P.T."

"What about the underwater vacuuming robot?"

"We're sending it back. They'll give me a fifty per-cent refund. So that's another four hundred ninety-nine dollars and ninety-nine cents. The ice-cream company will pick up their swirl-cone dispenser next week. No more free ice cream poolside . . ."

I swallowed hard. "What about giving out towels and water bottles and stuff? Is Johnny still doing that?"

Mom shook her head. "Johnny quit. He heard we were having financial trouble, so he took a job over at the Sea Spray."

She reached under the breakfast table and handed me a sweat-stained baseball cap and a walkie-talkie.

Yep.

I was officially the Wonderland's brand-new cabana boy.

Fool Boy

Around noon, my best buds from school—Pinky, Kip, and Porter—dropped by the pool for a dip.

I noticed that the new girl, Gloria Ortega, was sitting poolside in a lounge chair. She was wearing big bug-eye sunglasses, shorts, and a bright yellow T-shirt. It looked like she was doing homework. She kept running numbers through a calculator and jotting down notes in the same kind of ledger Mom keeps in her office. It was extremely weird. Who sits by the side of a swimming pool and does math problems?

Fact: swimming pools are not supposed to be study halls.

Since we didn't have many other paying guests (maybe six college students, plus two families with toddlers who, judging by their strange smiles, were definitely not obeying the We Don't Swim in Your Toilet, So Please Don't Pee in Our Pool sign), there was plenty of room in the sparkling water for my three buds to thrash through a couple of rounds of Marco Polo. Gloria rolled her eyes when the guys splashed water out of the pool onto her calculator.

Yep.

Yep. Two more dives like that and the pool will be completely empty.

She closed up her ledger book and stomped away, saying to one of the college girls, "I'll show you how to set up that Excel homework tracker for your MBA later, Dawn."

Unfortunately, I couldn't really join in the fun with Pinky, Kip, and Porter, because of my new pool-boy duties. While they played Marco Polo and jousted with pool noodles, I skimmed leaves out of the water with a net on a pole. When I was done doing that, I needed to scrub the sides of the pool.

Skimming and scrubbing used to be Pool Boy Johnny's jobs.

Now, of course, they were mine.

I also had to tote warm beach towels from the hot dryer in the laundry room to the even hotter (and unventilated) towel hut. Constantly. Why did people need so many towels? Did they use a different one for each toe? Anyway, since we were enjoying a freakishly high end-of-March temperature of eighty-two degrees with 82 percent humidity, by noon I had a freakishly bad case of B.O.

Another cold, hard fact: when the sun shines in the Sunshine State, Florida turns into a steam bath.

"Yo," said the Kipster, seeing the Out of Order sign Mom had hung on the ice-cream dispenser, "what's wrong with it?"

"It was swirling ice cream the wrong way," I told him.

"Seriously?"

"Yep. The nozzle is backward. We had counterclockwise spiraling action instead of the standard clockwise movement."

"So?"

"So counterclockwise ice cream never tastes as rich and creamy as the clockwise stuff."

Pinky Nelligan was nodding. "I thought something was a little off with that ice cream. I didn't want to say anything at the time. . . ."

"So who was that girl with the calculator?" asked Porter. "She was kind of cute. That's why I splashed water at her."

"Her name is Gloria Ortega," I told him. "Her dad's new on the sports crew at channel ten, WTSP."

"Awesome," said Kip, who's a total sports nut.

"Speaking of sports," hollered Pinky, "jump in, P.T. We need four players to make this an official chicken fight!"

I was wearing my bathing suit, so I was definitely tempted. I could peel off my Wonderland polo, kick off my sneakers, and dive into the refreshing blue water. Have I mentioned how hot it was?

But as much as I would've loved to cool off, I couldn't join in the fun. There was serious pool scum to be scrubbed.

As you might've guessed, I really wasn't looking forward to doing that job all by myself. It's a lot of work. Plus, you have to hold your breath when you clean the tiles underwater. Chlorine stings my eyes.

But with three friends lending a hand . . .

Yep. I was having another one of my famous brainstorms.

Scrub-a-Sub-Dub

"So, guys," I said to Pinky, Kip, and Porter, motioning for them to scoot over to the side of the pool, "don't stare or anything, but see those three college dudes over there? The ones with all the muscles?"

"Sure," said Porter. "What about them?"

"I heard them talking earlier." I looked around to make sure no one was listening, and lowered my voice. "They're not really in college. They're Navy SEALs."

"SEALs?" blurted Pinky. "No way! That is so awesome."

"Shhh! Dial it down a notch. They're only on a short break between secret missions. We don't want to blow their cover."

"Sure, sure," whispered Pinky.

"What are they doing here?" whispered Porter.

"Looking for guys our size."

"Really?" said Kip. "Why?"

"Because they're all too big."

"For what?"

I looked around suspiciously again. "Certain stealthy underwater *missions.*"

Pinky, Kip, and Porter looked at each other. Then they looked at me eagerly—the way puppy dogs do when they have no idea what you want them to do but they want to do it anyway.

"Just look at the muscles on that one guy," I said, nodding toward the college guy who looked like he was majoring in bodybuilding arts and sciences. "No way could he slip into a tight sewer pipe. He's too wide. But guys our size? We could do it easy."

"And sewer pipes lead everywhere!" said Kip.

"Sewer pipes and air-conditioning ducts," added Porter. "Spies use them in the movies all the time."

"Those three SEALs are here on a scouting mission," I told my friends.

"They're looking for baseball players?" asked Pinky.

"No! Talented individuals of a certain size who can hold their breath and do stuff underwater."

"What kind of stuff?" asked Porter.

"Tasks. Chores. Anything that requires stamina and a good pair of lungs." I used my foot to slide my bucket full of scrubbing tools closer to the lip of the pool. "Maybe even scrubbing the sides of a swimming pool. It doesn't really matter. If any of those guys see kids our size with potential, they're supposed to radio their commanding officers immediately."

"Hey," said Pinky, "what exactly are you doing with that bucket full of brushes, P.T.?"

"Just another one of my chores," I said with a sigh. "Mom told me I needed to, you know, dive in and scrub the sides of the pool sometime today, so—"

"So you waited until the Navy SEALs got here?" said the Kipster, like he just figured out what I was up to.

I shrugged. "Maybe."

"You think you're the only one around here who wants to go on top-secret commando sewer missions with Navy SEALs?" Porter asked angrily.

He reached up, grabbed a brush, and dove under the water.

Pinky and Kip were right behind him.

"Hey, you guys! You took all the brushes! No fair!"

"Maybe the SEALs need a leaf skimmer, too. Show 'em what you've got, P.T.," cracked Kip before plunging underwater.

So my friends scrubbed the sides of the pool for me.

I ambled over to ask the biggest muscleman for a little help.

"Excuse me, sir. Do you know how to work a walkie-talkie?"

"Well, duh."

"Can you show me?"

The guy grabbed my radio and pressed the button.

"Breaker, breaker, one-nine," he said, cracking up his friends. "Do you have your ears on?"

A voice crackled out of the speaker: "What? Who is this?" Grandpa. "Identify yourself. Over."

"Say you're calling for P.T."

The college guy jabbed the talk button again. "I'm calling for P.T."

"Oh, I see him." Grandpa waved at me from the window of his workshop. "Come on in, P.T. It's lunchtime. Over."

That's when my three friends bobbed up to the surface of the pool, proudly brandishing their brushes.

They climbed out just in time to hear the muscular "Navy SEAL" send a very important radio transmission to his commanding officer: "Roger that, sir. Ten-four. Over and out."

I went to join the guys.

"Wow," said Pinky. "Was he just talking to his boss?"

"I think so," I said.

"Awesome," said Kip. "We're going to be supersecret sewer spies!"

I grinned.

You see how powerful a story can be?

Sometimes, if you tell it just right, it'll even do your chores for you.

Baloney

"**I** heard them say they have to check out some other motels," I told the guys as the "Navy SEALs" and their friends drifted away from the pool. "But I think you guys definitely have a shot."

"Awesome!" said Pinky.

"Yeah," I said, pretending to be bummed, "for you three."

"You snooze, you lose," said Porter, because he always says annoying stuff like that. Sometimes he even rhymes.

"So," said Pinky, probably feeling sorry for me, "you wanna go grab lunch? We saw the Johnny Meatballs food truck cruising Gulf Boulevard."

"No thanks," I said. "I have to meet with my grandfather." I gestured toward his workshop near the pool.

I didn't want to tell the guys the truth: I didn't have any money for lunch, and I still needed to pass out towels and bottled water for the rest of the afternoon.

"Grandpa and I are discussing what new attractions we should install."

"Frisbee golf!" said Kip. "I keep telling you, P.T., you guys could lay out an insane Frolf course on your property!"

"I'll mention it to Grandpa. And if you guys hear from the Navy . . ."

"We won't tell you!" said Pinky. "Because it's supposed to be a top-secret operation!"

I shot him a wink. "Exactly."

"Catch you later, P.T.," said Porter as the three of them sloshed off in their wet bathing suits to go chase down the meatball truck.

When I was sure they were gone, I went to the towel heap the college kids had left behind and picked up my walkie-talkie.

"Grandpa? This is P.T. Do you, uh, have your ears on?"

"Ten-four. Over."

"So, what's for lunch? I'm starving. Over."

"Bologna and yellow mustard on white bread. Over."

"Again? Over."

"It's soft, P.T. At my age, softness is a very

important food feature. I have Cel-Ray soda, too. Over."

"I'll take a sandwich. You can have my soda. Over."

At least the workshop was indoors. That meant it would be shady. Too bad it didn't have air-conditioning.

"If I wanted to live inside a refrigerator my whole life," he'd say if I complained, "I'd be a hard-boiled egg!"

Shirts sweat-glued to our backs, Grandpa and I sat down on wooden crates filled with dusty memorabilia. A cardboard shipping box was our table. Through the window, I could keep my eye on the swimming pool and the gurgling frog slide. I noticed that Grandpa was finished painting the toothy smile on his Hawaiian Happy-Stinky Fruit.

Grandpa pulled a bologna sandwich wrapped in wax paper out of the crinkled brown paper grocery bag he toted his lunch in to the workshop every day. I think he's the only guy alive who still uses wax paper instead of ziplock bags.

I was so hungry that the sandwich—which turned into a bologna dough ball on the roof of my mouth—actually tasted pretty good.

"Don't tell your mother, but I bopped you a free Coke."

He handed me a frosty glass bottle. Yep. At the

Wonderland, we still have Coke in bottles, not cans. Dr. Brown's Cel-Ray, on the other hand, is like tuna fish. It only comes in cans.

"We probably shouldn't be taking free stuff from the vending machines anymore, Grandpa."

"Don't worry so much, kiddo. We Wilkies are like cats. We always land on our feet."

"But the banker . . ."

"Banker, schmanker. Don't worry about it. When we beat Disney World and become the 'Hottest Family Attraction in the Sunshine State,' our money worries will be over."

"Awesome," I said. "When, exactly, is the contest?"

"Voting starts in June. Just in time for family vacation season. The winner will be announced in August."

"This is March."

"Yep. Only five more months to go!"

I didn't have the heart to tell Grandpa that August would be way too late.

We didn't have five months.

We had less than four weeks.

Making Magic

"**W**e just need to drum up a little extra business is all," said Grandpa. "Fill all the rooms."

"Okay. But how?"

"Well, back in the day, I used to put on my red-striped jacket, grab my megaphone, and work Gulf Boulevard like a carnival barker. Oh, I had some good patter, P.T. Good patter . . .'"

Pull right in, folks. You will be amazed and astounded by the seven wonders of Walt Wilkie's Wonder World.

See Dino, the dinosaur that ate Milwaukee. Ride the galloping jackalope. Send your family to the moon!

"We could do it again," said Grandpa. "We already have the steak. All we need is a little sizzle."

"Huh?"

"We have all the bigger-than-life characters. We have a rocket ship and a giant dinosaur. We just have to turn them into something bigger than molded fiberglass and paint."

"And, uh, how do we do that?"

"P.T., tell me: what makes Walt Disney World so special?"

"Um, *everything*?"

"Nope, nope, nope. It's the stories. Why do kids want to meet all those Disney princesses at the castle? Because they know their fairy tales backward and forward before their families even pull into the parking lot. Pirates of the Caribbean? That ride tells such a great story they turned it into four different movies."

"But we don't have those kinds of attractions. We just have a bunch of statues."

"So? If you didn't know him from his cartoons, what's Mickey Mouse except a large rodent who likes to dress up in human clothes? Dino, the dinosaur out front? I used to tell folks he was the sole survivor of a prehistoric ice age. That he fell asleep in an arctic glacier, thawed out during the heat wave of 1963, and made his way down to Milwaukee because—little-known fact—dinosaurs love bratwurst! He also had a hankering for cheese. 'Gouda cheese, not the bad-a stuff.' That line always earned me a few chuckles."

"A dinosaur who crawled out of his glacier so he could head down to Milwaukee for sausage and cheese?"

"Exactly! See, I wanted to tie my story in with the Morty D. Mouse statue out back. Since I bought that statue from a gourmet cheese shop outside Sheboygan, Morty already had the cheese wedge and the sausage link."

"That's ridiculous, Grandpa."

"No, P.T., it's fun. You stage that kind of silliness down here in Florida, and—bingo—you just created a little 'fun in the sun,' which is exactly what all those folks getting off the airplanes in Orlando and Tampa are looking for. The wonders and marvels they just can't find in the cold gray slush of everyday life."

Grandpa put down his sandwich and soda. He rummaged in a box and found a faded comic book–style brochure with Dino on the cover.

"Tourists from Wisconsin? They loved hearing about Dino and the cheese. They could relate."

"What about everybody else?"

Grandpa sighed. "They just wanted to have some fun. See their kids smile. And, at the very end of my spiel, when I hit the play button on my eight-track tape deck and Dino roared? Everybody screamed like they were on a roller coaster."

Grandpa laughed, remembering it all. That made me smile.

When he was all laughed out, he belched up another cloud of Cel-Ray salad gas.

"Of course," he said, rubbing his face, "no one wants to hear my corny old stories anymore."

"But it used to work?"

"Like a hot knife through presliced butter. Because everybody needs a little wonder in their lives, P.T. That's why vacations were invented. To give us room for amazement!"

I was smiling up until Grandpa used the word "room."

It made me remember how many of ours were empty.

Freddy the Frog

Grandpa's speech made me wonder (pun intended): would his corny old stunts still work?

Were people still hungry for marvels and stories and wonders to behold—stuff they didn't have back home because they were too busy going to school or working or raising a family?

If Grandpa's stories were a little out of date, could I come up with some funny new ones?

I checked my watch. Our lunch break was almost over. It was time for a crazy new idea.

"You have your walkie-talkie, right, Grandpa?"

"Sure."

"And you can see the pool . . ."

"I hope so. It's right out the window, P.T."

"Can you do a good frog voice?"

"You mean like dis?" He sounded like a frog from New Yawk.

"Perfect. Go to channel three on your walkie-talkie. We may not want Mom listening in on this."

We both twisted our channel knobs.

I went to the clothes rack and grabbed his faded red-striped jacket. I rummaged around a little and found Grandpa's old bullhorn and straw hat. It was two sizes too big and wobbly on my head, but it would work.

"P.T.?" Grandpa asked with the old twinkle back in his eyes. "What exactly are we going to do?"

"It's sizzle time!"

● ● ●

Grandpa put fresh batteries into the megaphone.

I pressed the talk button.

It squealed with feedback.

When nobody was looking (okay, there were only about eight people hanging out around the pool, and most of them were napping or flapping their water wings), I hid my walkie-talkie inside the mouth of the frog slide.

Once everything was in place, I nodded to Grandpa, who was watching from his workshop window.

He nodded back.

I clicked on the bullhorn and started babbling.

"Ladies and gentlemen, boys and girls, this

is your pool attendant, P. T. Wilkie, speaking. Welcome to the Wonderland, the most amazing motel on Florida's Gulf coast. Home to marvels to behold and stories to be told! No, I'm not talking about my grandfather or even Cheeseball the cat. I'm talking about Freddy the Frog."

I gestured grandly to the gurgling waterslide.

"Now, I couldn't help but notice that earlier today, some of you kids were brave enough to actually climb inside Freddy's mouth and slide down his slippery tongue. How many of you did that?"

The five kids gawking up at me from the shallow end of the pool all raised their hands.

"And I'm gonna do it again," said a boy.

"You are?" I said through the megaphone so Grandpa could hear me. "Well, Freddy, what do you think about that?"

Grandpa, ever the showman, picked up on his cue.

"You try it, kiddo," grumbled a voice from inside the frog, "and I might have to eat youse."

The kid's eyes opened wide.

"Now, Freddy," I said, "that's not nice. These children are our guests."

"I know, I know. But I ain't had no breakfast this mornin'. And guests taste better than flies."

A girl in a pink bathing suit padded around the edge of the pool and propped her hands on her hips.

"Is that frog really talking?"

"I think he's really talking," I said.

"I think I'm really talking, too!" snapped Grandpa.

I handed the megaphone to the little girl. "You're not real," she shouted at the frog.

"Oh, yes I am," crackled Grandpa through the walkie-talkie. "I'm green, ain't I?"

I took back my megaphone.

"Ladies and gentlemen, boys and girls, Freddy here is what marine biologists call a talking sea frog. Yes, he may seem a little stiff, but that's because talking sea frogs don't move around much once the sun is up. If they stay perfectly still, they think nobody can see them."

"I'm blending in here," said Grandpa. "Disappearing amidst the flora and fauna."

"Freddy hopped out of the ocean because he likes to drink swimming-pool water. It tastes a lot better than the salt water in the ocean, which, as you might imagine, can be very salty."

"That's right," said Grandpa in his gravelly frog voice. "I prefer this water right here. So don't pee in the pool. I ain't interested in drinking lemonade! By the way, kid, I love your pink bathing suit."

Now the girl's father was up, laughing and aiming his cell phone at the scene.

"You can see my bathing suit?" the girl said with a gasp.

"Of course I can," said Freddy the Frog. "Why do you think I have such big eyes? So I can see stuff."

"How many fingers am I holding up?"

"Two."

"Nuh-uh. This is three."

"I know. Two fingers and one thumb."

Everybody around the pool cracked up.

"So, Freddy," I say, "what's your favorite year?"

"Leap year, of course," answered Grandpa, because he's the one who taught me that corny joke in the first place. "And do you know why I like to go to the mall?"

"No, Freddy. Why?"

"I like to go hopping. You know what I order every time I go to Burger King?"

"No," I said, playing along. (I think Grandpa might've memorized a frog joke book back in the day.)

"French flies and a diet croak."

We did this back-and-forth bit for maybe five minutes. The kids laughed their heads off.

The parents were smiling, happy to see their kids having so much (you guessed it) fun in the sun.

"Excuse me," one of the fathers said to me.

"Yes, sir?"

"Do you guys do this comedy routine every day?"

"You bet. Rain or shine."

He nodded and talked to somebody on his cell. "You should definitely switch motels, Charlie. They got these free shows and stuff for the kids. It's a nice amenity."

Then he handed me a twenty-dollar bill.

What do you know?

Grandpa and I just earned our first tip.

If we kept this up, we'd have that bank loan paid off in, oh, a little over a decade.

There's No Business Like Frog Business

Apparently, Gloria Ortega had been watching our frog show from up on the second-floor balcony.

She came down the stairs and handed me a dollar bill.

"Add it to your tips," she said.

Sweet. Now we had twenty-*one* dollars.

"You guys are good," she said.

"Thanks."

"You do this all the time?"

"Well, my grandfather used to. I'm kind of new to it."

"Can I be honest with you . . . uh . . ." She hesitated because I'd never told her my name.

"P.T.," I said.

"Petey?"

"No. Pee. Tee."

"You're kidding. Like P. T. Barnum? The show-man, hoaxer, and all-around huckster who never said, 'There's a sucker born every minute,' even though everybody thinks he said it? I did a report on him last year. He was a very smart business-man. Nailed the whole concept of personal brand-ing before anybody else even called it that."

"That's the guy," I said. "He also started the Bar-num and Bailey Circus. He's kind of a hero to me and Grandpa."

"So your name is Phineas Taylor Wilkie?"

"I prefer P.T."

"So would I. Speaking of suckers . . ."

She bobbed her head toward the second floor. The six college kids were coming out of their rooms.

"Lose the goofy striped jacket and hat," said Gloria.

"What?"

"Trust me. It's the wrong image if you want to appeal to the college-aged demographic. Not at all cool."

"Oh, really? Says who?"

"Me. And anybody else with eyeballs. Hurry. You need to do a second show."

"How come?"

"Because those college kids have friends, and you have rooms to fill."

"What? How do you—"

"Motel capacity is extremely easy to monitor, Phineas. Your Vacancy sign is still lit. Whereas the 'No' neon is so dusty, if you ever did turn it on, no one would see it."

"Are you, like, a detective or something?"

"No," said Gloria. "Not to brag, but I'm a business wiz. And frankly, right now I'm also extremely bored. I wouldn't mind investing in your roadside attraction start-up."

"You mean you'd give us money?"

"Sure. I'd love to. But I don't have any. I mean, I would if I played the stock market with real money instead of, you know, just pretend digits on paper. This morning, my portfolio was up fifteen percent. I'm a billionaire. Or, you know, I would be . . ."

"If you had any real money."

"Right. But what I've got, P.T., is business smarts. Savvy. Acumen. The know-how you need to move on from the low-hanging fruit and start drinking water from a fire hydrant."

"Huh?"

"It's business talk, P.T. Work with me. Now get your frog talking again. Better yet, let's hear it sing. We need to hook those suckers—I mean, college kids."

"How about we do a little Croaky Karaoke?"

Gloria snapped her fingers and shot me double-digit pistols. "I like it, I like it!"

I grabbed the walkie-talkie out of the frog's mouth.

"You ready for round two, Grandpa?"

"Roger that and ten-four, good buddy. This is fun. Like back in the day."

"Great. Do you know that song 'Take Me to the River'? The one Big Mouth Billy Bass sings on TV?"

"Know it? I have one of those fish hanging on the wall back here."

"Great. Wait for your cue. Gloria?"

"Yeah?"

"Stand by to sing along with Freddy."

"What?"

"You're my first pretend customer."

The college kids were headed toward the parking lot.

"Here you go, little lady," I said to Gloria through the bullhorn. "The megaphone is yours. Sing along with Froggy!"

Grandpa started singing a very froggy version of Big Mouth Billy Bass's greatest hit: *Take me to da river . . .*

Gloria Ortega sang along: *Drop me in the water!*

Then they destroyed the next verse and chorus.

The college kids thought it was such a goof they forgot where they had wanted to go and paid ten dollars each to sing along with Freddy the Frog.

So did some of the parents and little kids. Especially when Grandpa added new songs to Freddy's repertoire: "Someday My Prince Will Come," "Bein' Green," and something called "Froggy Went A-Courtin'" that only Grandpa and a college kid from New Jersey knew the words to.

By the time we were done, we had over one hundred dollars stuffed inside a sand bucket that a six-year-old had let me borrow.

And the college kids were texting all their friends, telling them to check out (and check in to) the Wonderland!

Frogonomics

Saturday evening, ten more of our rooms were booked.

Most of the new guests asked Mom when "the next frog show" would be.

Good thing I was there in the lobby.

"All day, on the hour, starting at eleven. Croaky Karaoke starts at three."

Mom just sort of looked at me.

When all the new paying customers were checked in, I explained what Grandpa, Gloria, and I were up to. I also gave Mom $117.49.

"For the balloon payment," I said. "Or you can just buy a bunch of balloons to decorate the lobby. Your choice."

She smiled. An actual tear welled up in the corner of one of her eyes. I think. Like I said, Mom never cries. But there was something moist glistening up there before she immediately wiped it away.

"Thanks, P.T.," she said. "Every little bit helps."

● ● ●

That night, Grandpa, Gloria, and I rigged up a better sound system for the frog.

We installed a speaker (so I could cue Grandpa with the walkie-talkie), a microphone connected to an amp and a pair of headphones (so Grandpa could hear people without me repeating everything through my bullhorn), and an old video camera (so Freddy, aka Grandpa, could see people better and say things about their clothes, their hair, their lack of hair, their complete baldness—whatever).

And, yes, it's amazing how many shoe boxes jammed with electronic junk and cables Grandpa had stockpiled in that workshop of his.

Fact: he has never thrown *anything* away.

"Correct me if I'm wrong," said Gloria when we were done rigging our gear, "but hasn't your motel been half empty since forever?"

"Yeah," I said. "More or less."

"So why the sudden push to increase cash flow?"

"Can I be totally honest with you?"

"You better be. Especially if we're going to be business partners."

"Are we?"

"I think so. I'm bored, remember?"

"Right. Okay. Five years ago, my grandpa took out a one-hundred-thousand-dollar loan on this motel, and now, all of a sudden, we have to pay off the whole thing in, like, twenty-nine more days."

Gloria nodded. "Your final balloon payment, so called because of its large size. You see, P.T., a balloon-payment mortgage is not fully amortized, or paid off, over the term of the note, thus there is a balance due at maturity."

Okay. That went right over my head. *WHOOSH!*

"How could you possibly know that?" I asked. "You're my age."

"You're twelve?"

I nodded.

"Cool. But it doesn't matter how old I am, P.T. Like I told you: I love this stuff! I'm a marketing maven. And guess what?"

"What?"

"That's exactly what you guys need."

Froggy Goes to Market

On Sunday morning, Gloria Ortega was brimming with new ideas.

"Merchandising, P.T. Marketing. These are things I learned about in J.A."

"What's that?"

"Junior Achievement. It's a school club where you learn how to unleash your entrepreneurial spirit and run your own business."

"Like on that TV show *Shark Tank*?"

"Sort of. See, we move around a lot. My dad's working his way up the dial, hopping from one TV station to another all over the country, hoping to one day make it to the big league: ESPN."

"Wow. That would be awesome."

"Yeah. It might also be impossible. But, hey, it's his dream. Anyway, whenever Dad needs to move to a new city, I always make sure the school where I'll be going has a J.A. program. Makes the transition easier if, at least *after* school, I'm going into semi-familiar territory."

"So what would J.A. do with Freddy the Frog?"

For an answer, Gloria dumped a shopping bag full of stuff she'd just bought from Dollar Bill's Discount Barn, a bargain store up the boulevard in the strip mall: one hundred rubber frogs, a Sharpie pen, and a jumbo bottle of all-natural green food coloring.

"The frogs were four for a dollar, or twenty-five cents each. We write the name 'Freddy' on the back with the marker and sell them for five dollars. Net profit? Four dollars and seventy-five cents per frog."

"Why would anybody pay five dollars for a twenty-five-cent toy frog?"

"It's not a toy frog, P.T. It's a memory."

Seemed Gloria and Grandpa thought the same way: people came to Florida for sunshine and magic they could remember long after winter blew into town again.

I had only one question for my new "business partner."

"And how much of that four-dollars-and-seventy-five-cents profit do you take home?"

"Just give me back my twenty-five cents per frog."

"Seriously?"

She shrugged. "Like I said, with no J.A. business to run until school starts, I'm extremely bored just sitting in my room making money on paper with my pretend stock portfolio. You know, I'd be a billionaire . . ."

"If you had any real money."

"Exactly. Besides, your mom is awesome. She's definitely role-model material."

"She is?"

"Hey, she's kept this old-school, retro motel running without ever flipping on the No Vacancy sign. That must've taken some kind of major money-shuffling miracle."

"Yep. According to Mom, that's why we call it the Wonderland: 'Because it's a wonder we're still open.'"

"But, P.T., you are. And somehow, she did it. Plus, not to get all mushy or anything, I sort of like the wacky decorations. There's a giant mouse nibbling sausage and cheese right outside my window."

"That's Morty D. Mouse. He hails from Sheboygan, Wisconsin, where he used to work at Ye Olde Cheese Shoppe."

"Hmmm. Maybe we could sell cheese. No. Scratch that. Bad idea. Wisconsin is cheese; Florida is chocolate-covered coconut patties."

"And orange juice."

"Right. We can add the Florida angle later. Let's stick with what we know is working: Freddy the Frog. Okay, big idea. Let me blue-sky it for you: We set up a digital camera and computer. Take 'official' photographs of folks posing with Freddy. Run them through my Print Shop app so we can add a 'My Friend Freddy the Frog' banner on the bottom. Then we email our customers the finished files. We could charge, I don't know, ten bucks a shot."

"Ten bucks? Do you think people will pay that much when they could just take a selfie?"

"They're on vacation, P.T. Their brains are taking the week off, too."

Wow, I thought. *Gloria's good.*

And she got my wheels spinning.

"We should print up copies of lyrics to all those songs Grandpa knows," I suggested. "It's easier to sing along with Freddy if you know the words."

"Perfect," said Gloria. "Way to be proactive."

"So, what's the bottle of green food coloring for?" I asked.

Gloria gestured toward the self-serve ice-cream machine. "Is that thing really out of order?"

"No. We just can't afford to give away free ice cream anymore."

"I agree. But you could sell it. Say three dollars a cone? And, P.T.?"

"Yeah?"

"It isn't ice cream."

"No?"

"Nope." She jiggled the jug of green food coloring. "It's Freddy the Frog's Frozen Green Pond Scum."

A New College Craze!

Who knew singing karaoke with a giant green frog could be such a huge hit?

Especially with college girls.

And wherever college girls go, college boys seem to follow.

Sunday afternoon, our pool was mobbed. Suddenly, it was *the* place to be on St. Pete Beach. We were so busy once the texts and tweets started flying I had to call Pinky Nelligan, Kip Rand, Porter Malkiel, *and* Julie Scarboro to ask them to lend a hand selling souvenirs.

They worked for free, too. All they wanted was a Frozen Green Pond Scum cone (and to watch all the big kids make fools of themselves).

Johnny, our former pool boy, who's a senior in high school, heard about all the college kids flocking to the Wonderland pool and begged Mom to give him his old job back.

"I'll take a pay cut," he told her.

Mom gave him exactly what he asked for.

My job? Well, since I didn't have to work up a sweat passing out towels anymore, I could concentrate on cooking up a story to make Freddy come alive.

"Ladies and gentlemen, there is a reason why Freddy the Frog wants you to take him to the river and drop him in the water. He figures after he's had a nice bath and splashed on a little cologne, he'll smell good enough for one of you young ladies to pucker up and kiss him on his extremely thin frog lips." I eyed some of the college guys. "And from the look of things, some of you ladies have had experience kissing frogs. . . ."

On one of our breaks, Grandpa came out of his workshop to beam at the crowd. His smile was so big he looked like one of those happy sun-head men wearing sunglasses you see all over Florida postcards. (I never figured out why the sun would need sunglasses, unless, I guess, he drifted past a mirror.)

"This is how it used to be, P.T.," he told me. "Never thought I'd see it again. Thanks, kiddo."

Then he tousled my hair.

Fact: he's the only one in America allowed to do that.

Mom loved what we were up to, and not just because we were raking in fistfuls of cash.

"This reminds me of when I was growing up

here at the motel," she told me when I nipped into the air-conditioned lobby between shows to rest my voice. "You're a lot like your grandfather, P.T. He used to make up all sorts of outrageously ridiculous stories. And guess what. I loved every single wonderful one of 'em!"

She leaned in and kissed me. *SMACK!* Right on the cheek.

"Sorry," I told her. "I didn't turn out to be a prince, either."

She smiled.

"Yes, you did, P.T. A long time ago."

"So . . . do I have to wear a crown and funny tights?"

"No. Please. Don't."

Mom took the money we'd collected so far into the office so she could lock it up in the safe.

That first haul was nearly one thousand dollars.

When the day was done, we'd raked in close to three!

"Not bad," said Gloria, my business partner and chief marketing advisor. "But, P.T.?"

"Yeah?"

"We need to do better. Much, much better."

Good News/Bad News

The pool pretty much cleared out around five o'clock.

Everybody was heading off to grab something to eat.

"Note to self," Gloria said to her iPhone, which I think had one of those note-taking apps. Either that, or she was just seriously strange. "Work out a deal with nearest pizza parlor to deliver frog-themed pies. 'Lily Pad' for pepperoni. 'Warts and All' for a pizza supreme with everything on it. 'Swamp Gas' for green peppers, garlic, and onions."

Gloria Ortega had business ideas the way Grandpa and I have story ideas.

"Why do you say we need to do 'much, much better'?" I asked after Pinky and the gang headed home. "We made nearly three thousand dollars.

We keep that up every day for a month, we'll take in ninety thousand dollars. All the increased room bookings should bring in at least another ten thousand bucks. That means by the end of April, we'll easily have the one hundred thousand dollars we need to pay off the banker."

"Your math is solid, P.T.," said Gloria.

"Thank you."

"But your logic stinks. How can we possibly keep doing this for a month?"

"There are other attractions," I told her. "If the singing frog bit becomes boring, we can move on to Dino the Dinosaur. . . ."

Gloria shook her head. "That's not my point, P.T. We need to make one hundred thousand dollars *this week*. School's back a week from tomorrow, remember? Spring Break will be over. Not just for us, but for most of these snowbirds and college kids, too."

"Well," I said, "other colleges take the next week off. Other families, too."

"So, what? You're going to play hooky for a month? Ask the nice police officers to do the voice of Dino the Dinosaur when they show up to haul your butt back to school?"

She had a point. Mom wouldn't let me skip classes for a whole month. It would look bad on my permanent record.

"Well, what can we do?" I asked.

"I don't know," said Gloria. "But don't worry. I'm working on it. Brainstorming a few notions that I hope to fast-track into concepts."

When we reached the office, Gloria's dad was casually leaning on the front counter, chatting with Mom, who had a dreamy sort of look in her eyes I had never seen before. Plus, she had taken off her glasses. Something weird was definitely going on.

"If you'll have us," said Mr. Ortega, "we'd like to book the room for a whole month."

"Oh, that's wonderful," said Mom, sounding a

little like Stephanie Gross, this girl at school who really, really, *really* likes boy bands.

I arched an eyebrow. Mom flipped back to her professional desk-clerk face.

"I mean, we'd be happy to have you, Mr. Ortega."

Mom clacked on her computer keyboard. Mr. Ortega smiled some more. I wondered if he painted his teeth with white shoe polish or something.

"We appreciate your hospitality, Mrs. Wilkie."

"Please," said Mom, "call me Wanda."

"The game is always tougher when you're on the road," said Mr. Ortega. "But Gloria and I don't really want to start house hunting until we're absolutely, one hundred and ten percent certain that WTSP is the right fit for me," he said. "I have another offer from a station in Boise, Idaho. I do love double-baked potatoes."

"Don't we all?" said Mom, sounding funny again. "Will Mrs. Ortega be coming down to help you two find your new, permanent home? I mean, if you decide to stay in St. Petersburg, of course."

"No," said Gloria very matter-of-factly. "My mom died five years ago. We were living in Scranton at the time."

Mr. Ortega nodded. "WNEP-TV 16." He said it like those were the saddest letters and number in the whole world.

"I'm sorry for your loss," said Mom.

"Thank you," said Mr. Ortega. "We miss her every day."

"So where's Mr. Wilkie?" asked Gloria. I could tell she wanted to change the subject. "I haven't met him yet."

"Yes, you have," I said. "Except I just call him Grandpa. I think he's taking a nap. All that singing kind of wore him out."

"I meant your father."

"Oh." I looked at Mom.

She answered for me.

"He isn't here, Gloria. P.T.'s father left a long, long time ago."

Yep.

It was so long ago I'd never even met the guy.

Big Ideas

That night, Gloria didn't ask me any more questions about my dad.

I was happy about that. Hate to say it, but the whole topic's sort of a buzzkill.

Instead, Gloria and I went to work. I took her on a tour of the Wonderland grounds so we could brainstorm, blue-sky, and spitball new attractions. (She was also teaching me some of her business buzzwords.)

"That used to be a Muffler Man," I said, pointing to the twenty-five-foot-tall fiberglass statue of a bearded guy in blue jeans and a red shirt. "Grandpa bought him from a tire-repair place up in Michigan years ago. He used to hold a muffler in his hands. That's why one palm's up and the other one's down like that. So he can hold stuff."

"Who's he supposed to be?" asked Gloria.

"Smilin' Sam is what Grandpa calls him."

"Why?"

"Beats me. But if we grab a ladder, we could paint his cap silver so it looks like a helmet. Then we could attach a bunch of fake feathers to the side and make it look even more like conquistador headgear. Add a plywood sword down the side of his pants, and—*BOOM!*—I could tell everybody he's Ponce de León.

"I'd say, 'Folks, Ponce de León never found the Fountain of Youth, but he definitely located the legendary Fountain of Tall.' We could bottle tap water and sell it to short guys who want to play basketball. Or we could play the history angle and book school visits. We just wouldn't tell Mr. Frumpkes."

"Cute," said Gloria. "But I think we need something bigger."

"Bigger? Hello? Did I mention that Ponce here is twenty-five feet tall?"

"I mean a bigger idea."

"All right," I said, moving around to the side of the motel. "How about the jackalope?"

I pointed to the statue of the giant jackrabbit with antelope horns. It had a saddle on its back that you could climb onto, cowboy-style. If you put a quarter in its money box, the jackalope rocked back and forth on its hind legs so you could pretend you were riding the fearsome critter like a bucking bronco.

"What do we do with him besides charge twenty-five cents per ride?" asked Gloria.

"Make up a story."

Gloria was shaking her head. "I think we need something better than just a story."

"*Just* a story? Might I remind you, Miss Ortega, that a story is what turned Freddy the Frog into a cash machine?"

"I know, Phineas. I was there. But to take this thing to the next level, we need a story *plus*."

"Plus what?"

"I don't know. Something interactive. Something that people can participate in—even if they're not staying at this motel. Something that'll grab the whole beach's attention."

"How about a jackalope hunt?" I suggested. "We could buy a bunch of Super Soakers . . ."

"And have people chase after a fiberglass statue that isn't running away from them?"

"Okay. Forget the jackalope hunt. How about a treasure hunt? We've got just the pirate for it."

"Where?"

"The Putt-Putt golf course."

"Show me."

He used to have a parrot on his shoulder. But it blew off during our last hurricane.

I led Gloria to the palm-and-grapefruit grove that shaded Grandpa's nine-hole miniature golf course. It was only about fifty feet away from the beach.

"That's the footlocker I took to camp once," I said, pointing at the pirate's treasure chest. "Grandpa painted it up like that when I told Mom how much I hated camp and never wanted to go back."

"Perfect!" said Gloria.

"You hated camp, too?"

"No. Actually, I've never been to camp. We move around too much. But the treasure chest is perfect. First thing tomorrow, we need to head back to Dollar Bill's Discount Barn."

"Grandpa will drive us," I said. "What will we be looking for?"

"Treasure. Enough spangly baubles and shiny trinkets to fill that box. We need a pair of sand shovels, too."

"You mean for making a sand castle?"

Gloria shook her head again. "Nope. The big kind. We need to bury some treasure!"

Ahoy, Me Hearties!

The next morning, Gloria, Grandpa, and I basically grabbed every kind of ten-cent toy we could find at Dollar Bill's Discount Barn.

Bouncy balls. Whistles. Clapping hands. Squiggly snakes. Wax lips. Vampire fangs. Fake money. Rub-on tattoos.

And lots of gold-foil chocolate pirate coins.

"Seriously?" said Gloria when I grabbed two bags, each loaded with two hundred shiny coins. "Four hundred years ago, pirates buried a treasure chest filled with chocolate under the hot Florida sand and it never melted?"

"Of course not. Pirate chests were always vacuum sealed," I told her.

"And extremely well insulated," added Grandpa. "They were the first ice chests."

"And you expect people to believe that the chocolate coins have been buried for hundreds of years because . . . ?"

"Because *we* believe it," said Grandpa. "That's how you sell a bit, Gloria. You believe in it. That's how you sold Freddy the Frog's Frozen Green Pond Scum."

"True," said Gloria.

"Besides," I added, "everybody loves chocolate. Nobody asks too many questions when they find it for free. And look at those skulls and crossbones stamped into the gold foil. Come on. That's pirate-y."

Grandpa nodded. "Very pirate-y. Downright buccaneerish."

"Fine," Gloria said with a laugh. "P.T.'s the one who has to make it sound believable."

"Trust me," I told her. "I'm very good at making fake stuff sound real."

Grandpa put his hand on my shoulder. "Taught the boy everything I know!"

After we shopped for treasure, we loaded up on plastic beach pail-and-shovel sets, even though all we really needed was the shovels. They were a dollar each. We bought a case—forty-eight buckets and shovels. Total cost for the pirate chest exhibit? One hundred three dollars and forty-six cents.

Our last stop was the grocery store, to pick up a couple of bags of Pirate's Booty. I thought the salty, cheesy snack would go well with all that chocolate.

Grandpa agreed. Gloria rolled her eyes (something she does so often I wondered if they were loose).

"Fine," she said. "Whatever. I believe, I believe."

Finally, we lugged all the loot back to the motel and started loading the chest inside Grandpa's workshop.

Well, Gloria and I did. Grandpa needed a nap.

I helped myself to a few of the chocolate gold coins. A couple of Pirate's Booty cheese curls, too.

"You know we can't use that bag now, right, P.T.?" said Gloria.

She was right. So I finished the whole bag.

"Come on, P.T.," said Gloria. "You can't keep eating the treasure before we bury it!"

"I'm not eating it. I'm plundering it."

"Whatever. Save some for the paying customers."

We finished stuffing the footlocker with loot and sealed it up tight.

"Once we bury the chest," I said, "we'll draw a map."

"Make sure you put in all sorts of twists and turns," said Gloria. "Make it easy but hard."

"Definitely. I'll work in some rhyming clues, too. Riddles the treasure hunters have to decipher."

"Perfect. Is there a copy machine in the office?"

"Yep. Mom said we can run off as many as we want."

Gloria whipped out her cell phone. It had a

calculator app. "If we sell the maps for five dollars each, we need to sell twenty-one to break even."

"What if we 'rent' the shovels for another five dollars?"

Gloria grinned. "Now you're catching on."

"We just have to make sure the maps look like they're worth five bucks."

"You can use this parchment paper," said Grandpa, coming into the workshop just as we were double-sealing the lid on the treasure chest with clear packing tape so sand wouldn't leak into it and turn the chocolate coins into round Nestlé Crunch bars.

"I thought you were taking a nap," I said.

"Who can nap when life is all of a sudden exciting again? Here. I bought this stuff years ago. See how it's sort of torn around the edges? I used it to print up scorecards for the Pirate Pete's Putt-Putt course—back when people liked to play Putt-Putt."

"It's perfect for a treasure map," I said. "*Extremely* pirate-y."

"Aye, that it is, matey," said Grandpa, squinting like he needed an eye patch. "Arrrrr!"

Gloria and I both laughed.

Grandpa dropped his pirate voice and said, "You kiddos are doing a fantastic job."

"Thanks," I said.

"Here," said Grandpa. "I want you each to have one of these. They're almost antiques." He handed us two old-fashioned, slightly faded postcards. "Thanks for keeping my dream alive, P.T. You too, Gloria."

"Well," I said, "we're trying, Grandpa."

"But we have a long way to go," added Gloria.

"Well, thank you, then, just for trying."

The old postcards were pretty awesome. They showed Walt Wilkie's Wonder World back in its glory days.

And Grandpa smiling. Just like he was now.

Digging Ourselves a Hole

Gloria and I waited until the sun set.

Then we trekked from the pirate statue (our starting point), around the pool, to where treasure hunters would have to pick up a clue from the Freddy the Frog's Frozen Green Pond Scum stand. We were hoping if it was a hot day, all the customers grabbing their clues would want to buy an ice-cream cone, too.

If they deciphered that clue, it would take them to the rocket ship, where, if they answered a riddle taped to one of its fins, they'd be told to go to the pink flamingo in the rear parking lot.

At the pink flamingo, they'd pick up a second map (my idea), which would lead them down to the beach and tell them to take a sharp left at the trash barrel, take a right ten paces later, then go east, away from the ocean, toward a short stockade fence penning in a bungalow's backyard.

"X marks the spot," I said, setting down the treasure chest so I could dig a hole that in the morning would be shaded by the fruit trees on the other side of the fence. (Okay. I was a little worried about the chocolate coins melting. Shade was a good idea.)

Gloria had been keeping detailed notes while I blocked out the course. They would serve as the outline for our two clue-filled treasure maps. The first one would be available in the motel lobby for just five bucks!

The beach was dark. No one was watching what we were doing except a pair of pelicans.

I had a garden shovel that I had borrowed from the groundskeeper's toolshed. We didn't really have a groundskeeper—just a guy who showed up with a riding lawn mower and a rake every other week. But maybe if the Wonderland really bounced back, we could hire the guy full-time and put in flower beds or topiaries shaped like unicorns and warthogs— the kind of stuff they have at Disney World!

"How deep should we bury it?" I asked.

"Not too deep," said Gloria. "But not too shallow, either."

"How about two feet?"

"Sounds good."

At Gloria's insistence, we had wrapped the whole

tightly sealed treasure chest inside a clear plastic recycling bag, "to keep all the creepy sand crawlers out of it," as she put it.

Fine. If we were burying plastic party favors, foil-wrapped candy coins, and a standard supermarket bag of Pirate's Booty, we'd sort of blown the whole "authentic pirate treasure" angle anyway.

I dug down two feet.

Together, Gloria and I lowered the loaded treasure chest into the hole. We shoveled and shoved sand back in. The second we were finished, a beam from a flashlight blinded me.

"What's going on back there?"

I recognized the voice.

"Uh-oh," I quickly whispered to Gloria. "That's Mr. Frumpkes. A teacher from school."

"Mr. Wilkie? I'm waiting for your answer. What are you doing with a shovel in my mother's backyard? Any exotic seashells you happen to find belong in *her* collection, not yours!"

"This is the beach," I said.

"Correction. This is the beach behind my mother's house." Mr. Frumpkes glared at me over the fence—I think. I couldn't really see his face with that flashlight frying my eyeballs, but come on—Mr. Frumpkes *always* glares at me.

"That doesn't mean she owns it," said Gloria, who, since she hadn't officially enrolled at Ponce de León Middle School yet, could say that kind of snarky thing to an off-duty teacher.

"Who are you?" asked Mr. Frumpkes, swinging his locomotive beacon over to blind Gloria.

"None of your beeswax."

"Oh, it's my beeswax, Missy Miss. I will not have juvenile delinquents vandalizing my mother's property."

"It's not her property," said Gloria. "It's a public beach. Your mother's property is on the other side of the fence."

"Oh. I see. You're a little legal beagle. Getting all technical with me. Well, Missy Miss, just because my mother has the misfortune of living down the block from that sorry excuse for a motel—"

"The Sea Spray?" I said, because it's one of our nearest neighbors. "I think it's pretty nice. Their pool's not as much fun as ours, but—"

"I was talking about the Blunderland," said Mr. Frumpkes. "Don't forget, Mr. Wilkie, I am a history teacher. I know all about your grandfather's past failures. The Wonderland is nothing but a bloated white elephant."

"Aren't all elephants kind of bloated?" I said. "And my grandfather is not a failure."

"Ha! He's been washed up ever since that other Walt, the successful one, opened *his* world of wonders over in Orlando."

I didn't know what to say. Mr. Frumpkes sort of had me there. I started fiddling with the shovel handle.

"Are you this bad when you teach school?" asked Gloria.

"I beg your pardon?" sniffed Mr. Frumpkes.

"Do you mess up your facts like this when you teach history?"

"I'll have you know, young lady—"

"Walt Wilkie's Wonderland Motel isn't a failure. If it were, how come it's being featured on TV first thing tomorrow morning?"

"Oh, really?" scoffed Mr. Frumpkes. "Are the cameras coming to record the authorities finally hauling the kooky old coot off to jail? What'd he do? Forget to pay his real estate taxes?"

"You'll see," said Gloria. "Just be sure you watch *Ten News This Morning* tomorrow, Mr. Grumpkiss."

"Frumpkes!"

"Whatever. Come on, P.T. We don't need some old lady's stinky seashells. Let's head for home."

Fact: Gloria Ortega is kind of scary when she gets mad like that.

Double fact: she's also kind of awesome.

We hiked down the beach toward the surf.

When we were beyond the reach of Mr. Frumpkes's flashlight, I said, "So, Gloria. How can you be so sure that channel ten is going to put the Wonderland on TV tomorrow morning?"

"Because that's where my dad works."

"I know. But . . ."

"You're going to be on their morning show. Live. Talking about the treasure hunt."

"I am? What time?"

"I don't know. First I have to pitch the story to my father."

"You think the TV station will really send somebody out to cover our treasure hunt?"

"They don't have to. Dad's already here!"

Live at Five

Did you know that some people watch local news at five o'clock in the morning?

Well, that's when the channel ten morning news show starts. A satellite van from the TV station pulled into our parking lot at four-thirty a.m. Mr. Ortega wanted to interview me, live, at five-twenty-five.

I don't usually get up before seven. But to be on TV? I'd get up before I even went to bed!

"Make sure you give the name of the motel a couple times," Gloria said, coaching me. "And stop yawning."

"Right."

"Remember to be polite. Courteous. Grown-ups like polite and courteous kids."

"You got it."

"And stop yawning!"

"Right."

Mom was up for what Mr. Ortega called the "live remote," too. She was cradling a thermos mug of coffee and acting giddy again. Maybe it was strong coffee with lots of sugar. Maybe it was the cameras. Or maybe it was Mr. Ortega. His teeth were bright and shiny—even at five a.m.

"This is so exciting," Mom gushed to Gloria's dad.

Grandpa was sleeping in. "It's your show, P.T.," he'd said when Gloria and I told him I was going to be on TV talking about the big treasure hunt. "Just give 'em the old razzle-dazzle."

"Right," I said.

But when we walked away from Grandpa's workshop, Gloria arched an eyebrow and said, "Razzle-dazzle? Does that mean he wants you to wear that red-and-white-striped jacket again?"

I laughed. "Don't worry. I won't."

In fact, I dressed for my broadcast debut in a simple Wonderland Motel polo shirt and tan shorts.

"I'm so happy they let you do this story even though it's not sports," Mom said to Mr. Ortega.

"They want me to do some human-interest features as part of my new job with the sports team," he told her. "And as a human, I find what these kids are doing here at the motel to be very interesting."

A woman toting a huge video camera climbed out of the van.

"We're live in fifteen seconds, Manny."

"Thank you, my friend." He turned to me. "You ready, P.T.?"

"Yes, sir."

"P.T.?" said Gloria.

"Yeah?"

"Would you puh-leeze stop yawning?"

32

Lights, Camera, Me

The camerawoman turned on an extremely bright light mounted to her rig.

Mr. Ortega cleared his throat, waggled his eyebrows, adjusted his sport coat, and tugged at his tie. Then he started chanting "Five frantic frogs fled from fifty fierce fishes" to warm up his lips and tongue.

Who do you guys usually interview this early in the morning?

Crickets.

Gloria slipped out of camera range to "live tweet" my TV appearance.

The camerawoman counted down from five with her fingers.

Mr. Ortega nodded and smiled at somebody on the other side of the lens, then said, "That's right, Buffy. While many local middle school students are spending their Spring Break sleeping in and slaying video-game monsters, young P. T. Wilkie is helping out here, at his family's motel, reviving the fun and excitement that, once upon a time, in a Florida far, far away, was part of Walt Wilkie's Wonder World—the Sunshine State's original magic kingdom. Tell me, P.T., what's today's wacky activity?"

"Well, sir," I said very politely, "here at the Wonderland Motel, 7000 Gulf Boulevard, there are always marvels to behold and stories to be told. Today we'll be hosting a pirate treasure hunt."

Mr. Ortega gave me a good TV-guy chuckle. "Heh, heh, heh. Is it real pirate booty?"

"Oh, yes, sir," I said, because we put those bags of Pirate's Booty cheese curls in the treasure chest. "This statue here? That's to commemorate Stinky Beard, the smelliest pirate on the seven seas."

"Who?"

"Stinky Beard, the first pirate to land on St.

Pete Beach. All the other pirates made fun of him because his beard stank. He always dribbled his clam chowder down his chin."

"And you know where Stinky Beard's treasure is hidden?"

"Yes, sir. It's somewhere under the sand near the Wonderland Motel, 7000 Gulf Boulevard. My grandfather, Walt Wilkie, found Stinky Beard's treasure map years ago but forgot where he hid it until yesterday."

"And now you're making that treasure map available to the general public?"

"That's right." I waved a copy of the parchment-paper map at the camera. "For the first time ever! Plus, we added in a few modern-day riddles and wrinkles to make the treasure quest even more challenging."

"Sounds like fun."

"And it's inexpensive, too. It only costs ten bucks for a map and a shovel."

"What's the grand prize?"

I smiled right at the camera lens. "Whoever finds Stinky Beard's treasure chest gets to keep everything they find inside. Plus, *everybody* gets to have a whole lot of fun in the sun!"

"When does this fun start?" asked Mr. Ortega.

"Nine o'clock. No early birds, please. Some of our guests like to sleep in."

Mr. Ortega chuckled and turned to talk directly into the camera. He also pulled an old-fashioned postcard out of his sport coat pocket.

"There you have it, Buffy. Young P. T. Wilkie, re-creating the kind of zany amusements this one-of-a-kind resort was famous for back in the 1970s, when it was Walt Wilkie's Wonder World."

He showed the postcard to the camera. It was the same one Grandpa had given to me and Gloria. I figured Gloria had given hers to her dad when she'd "pitched the story" to him.

"For Channel Ten News, this is Manny Ortega. Keep your sunny side up!"

"We're clear," said the camerawoman.

"That means we're off the air," explained Mr. Ortega.

"And," said Gloria, thumbing her smartphone as she strolled over to rejoin us, "we are also off the charts. My tweet about the treasure hunt is being re-tweeted like crazy!"

"The studio loved the segment," reported the camerawoman, touching her earpiece. "Our Facebook page is lighting up with requests for more information."

That's when it hit me.

"We're going to need more treasure maps."

Fun in the Sun

You wouldn't believe the number of people who showed up for the treasure hunt.

Hundreds. Maybe a thousand.

Lots showed up at nine o'clock sharp. Lucky for us, no one found the buried treasure right away. So more treasure hunters kept trickling in.

It helped, of course, that it had been a slow news day and channel ten replayed snippets of my interview on all its morning newscasts. Also, Gloria kept sending out tweets.

My job was to make the whole thing fun.

"Don't get too close, folks," I told the crowd gathered around the pirate statue, "or you might learn why they called this bean-burrito-loving pirate Stinky Butt when they weren't calling him Stinky Beard!"

Everybody laughed. So I, of course, kept going.

"As you can see, ladies and gentlemen, Stinky Beard lost one leg and one hand during his years of swashbuckling. He also lost about five hundred pirate hats. They kept blowing off. And if he tried to catch them, he'd just hook himself in the head."

We sold five hundred treasure maps and rented out the sand shovels five hundred times. We also sold a lot of Freddy the Frog's Frozen Green Pond Scum ice cream and Stinky Beard's Grisly Green Grog. (Pinky Nelligan came up with the idea for the gloppy slop when some Green Pond Scum ice cream melted in a bowl.) Meanwhile, Mom and Gloria kept running back to Dollar Bill's Discount Barn to buy souvenirs we could resell. Because the Tampa Bay Buccaneers is our local NFL team, there was plenty for them to choose from: pirate flags, pirate eye patches, even bobblehead pirate dolls.

Arr. Shiver me timbers.

That's what me matey said after he put his wooden leg in the freezer.

All in all, we took in close to six thousand dollars.

More important, people had a blast following the clues and digging holes in the sand. The beach was so cratered it looked like the bright side of the moon. The college kids spent most of their time laughing, calling each other "dude," and flinging "sandballs" at each other. Grandpa dressed up like a pirate and entertained the youngest kids.

A sixth grader from Canada and his sister found the buried treasure chest around four o'clock and shared some of their gold chocolate coins with everybody else.

The treasure-hunt stunt also attracted a whole bunch of new guests who wanted to book a room at "such a wonderfully fun motel."

Early in the evening, Mr. Ortega and his camerawoman came back to the Wonderland to do a follow-up on the treasure hunt. He interviewed a lot of the guests, including a senior citizen who had just flown up from Miami.

"Name's Bob Jones," he told Mr. Ortega. "I'd always heard about Walt Wilkie's Wonder World. In fact, a young lady friend of mine once sent me a postcard from here."

Mr. Jones, who sported a pencil mustache and looked like he was about Grandpa's age, showed the camera a postcard that looked exactly like the ones Grandpa had given to Gloria and me. From where I was watching the interview, I could see the back of the old man's postcard. It had scribbling all over it and—gross—a big lipstick smooch plastered on top of the stamp.

"Didn't know if the place still existed," Mr. Jones continued. "But then I saw that young boy on TV down in Miami. Made my day."

Wow, I thought. *They even ran my silly story about Stinky Beard down in south Florida?*

"And," said Mr. Ortega to the camera, "Mr. Jones from Miami definitely picked up a win today, Tiffany. He booked the Wonderland Motel's last available room!"

That's right. For the first time since 1970-something, Grandpa flipped on the "No" part of our No Vacancy sign.

We were completely sold out!

Egging Each Other On

Wednesday morning we went back to Croaky Karaoke, but to be honest, the crowds were a little thinner.

To make matters worse, one family checked out of the motel. Our Pirate Chest Treasure Quest had been "too loud." We'd woken up their baby. Long story short, that "No" part of our No Vacancy sign wasn't lit very long. Not even twenty-four hours. We barely burned the dust off its neon tubing.

"We need a new gimmick," said Gloria after we did the nine a.m. Freddy show for that old guy, Mr. Jones, and a couple of kids splashing around in the pool, who told the frog to "shut up, please," because "Take Me to the River" was making it hard for them to hear each other screaming "Marco" and "Polo."

"We should do another treasure hunt," I suggested. "That's been our biggest moneymaker. We could restock the treasure chest with chocolate coins and—"

Gloria shook her head. "We need something brand-new, P.T. That's the problem with marketing stunts. People move on. They look for the next big thing. You can't sell a lot of heart-shaped boxes of Valentine's chocolates on February fifteenth. It's yesterday's news."

"Well, how about we give the treasure-hunt idea a fresh twist?"

"Go on. I'm listening."

"We do it like an Easter egg hunt. But—and this is what makes it huge—it's a *dinosaur* egg hunt." I cocked my thumb at the big statue of Dino looming over the parking lot.

"Do we bury this egg in the sand again?" asked Gloria. "Because that's a big yawn. Been there, done that, got the T-shirt *and* the eye patch."

"No holes. We hide the grand prize, the biggest plastic Easter egg we can find, somewhere here on the property or out on the beach—not buried but maybe behind something."

"We could toss it over Mrs. Frumpkes's fence," joked Gloria.

"Nah. She might bake the kids who found the egg into gingerbread cookies or something."

"But how do we make this event pop?" asked Gloria, stroking her chin and pacing.

"Easy," I said. "We make sure our humongous plastic egg is filled with something really cool. Not candy or trinkets from Dollar Bill's Discount Barn. This time, we give away a brand-new Xbox— preloaded with a Jurassic: The Hunted dinosaur video game."

"We do that, we're incurring significant start-up costs, P.T."

"True. But we need a prize we can brag about."

"Fine," said Gloria. "Cost of doing business. We'll take it out of the nine thousand four hundred eighty-five dollars and thirty-nine cents we've taken in so far."

I guess while I'd been doing stuff like eating and sleeping, Gloria had been doing stuff like crunching numbers.

"We should also hide a couple dozen smaller eggs filled with smaller prizes," I said. "We can scatter them all over the property. That way, we have lots of winners. When people see winners, they want to play, too."

"Okay," said Gloria. "This might work. But we need a hook. An angle."

"It's Dino's birthday party! He just turned sixty-five million years old."

"Huh," said Gloria. "Guess he can finally retire."

I laughed and kept tossing out ideas. "We decorate the whole motel with balloons. Maybe get a Barney the purple dinosaur cake from the supermarket. We see if Grandpa can dress up in safari clothes and a pith helmet like he's an archaeologist on a dig. . . ."

"I like it," said Gloria. "But we don't 'decorate' with balloons. We sell them. We sell the cake, too. A dollar a slice. And Grandpa charges to have his picture taken with kids, Santa-style."

Jazzed and totally pumped, we hiked to the parking lot to check out the fiberglass dinosaur statue. It was kind of dusty and dingy.

"We should probably hose him down," I said.

"Definitely. We don't want the star of our show looking gross and grungy."

I was about to go grab the hose when a convertible pulled into the parking lot.

The man in the dark suit was behind the wheel.

He had a passenger.

That guy was wearing a dark suit, too.

Both of them were checking their hairdos in the rearview mirror. The Wonderland was about to have another alligator attack. But this time, the gators were sharks!

Vulture Watch

Since Gloria and I are kids, we were basically invisible to the two adults blabbing in the car.

They kept yakking at each other, not at all worried that we were hearing every single word they said.

"We'll take possession in just over three weeks," said the man I recognized as Mom's banker. "No way will the Wilkies be able to scrape together one hundred thousand dollars to satisfy their balloon payment. It'll pop, right in their faces."

All of a sudden, I wasn't so eager to do the balloons for Dino's birthday party. They'd just be colorful reminders of how much money we owed the bank.

"How about all this other junk?" said the slick-looking man in the convertible's passenger seat. I think he combed his hair with motor oil. "The giant dinosaur. That ridiculous rocket ship. And what's that thing on the roof?"

"A rooster. I think. No. Wait. Could be a court jester. You know—the clowns with the funny hats. But don't worry, Arnold. You can knock it all down. Maybe sell some of the pieces to kooks who collect this kind of garbage."

I guess the banker thought Grandpa was some kind of a kook. And that his life's work was nothing but "garbage."

Well, call me a kooky garbage lover, but I thought the Wonderland's art collection was totally awesome-tastic. Okay, maybe it wasn't art, but it sure was fun. No way could we let two land sharks in dark suits tear it all down.

"I'm definitely demolishing the whole motel," said Arnold, who I figured might be some kind of big-deal real estate developer. We have a lot of those in Florida. "It screams '1965'! I'll replace it with Florida's finest, most spectacular, most magnificent modern beachfront condo complex."

"That would be huge, Arnold. Huge."

"Hey, if you have to think, why not think big? I'm talking high-rise. Fifteen, maybe twenty stories tall. Block everybody else's ocean view. Fancy appliances and shiny granite countertops in all the kitchens. I could sell the units for two, three million each, easy."

"We'll be happy to partner with you on that, Arnold," said the banker.

"You can handle all the mortgages."

"Sweet," joked the banker. "We're bankers. We love us some mortgages."

"So how much longer do these Wilkie people have to scrape together the one hundred K?"

"Twenty-five days. And believe me, there's no way these penny-ante pikers are capable of raising that kind of cash that quickly."

Gloria had overheard enough.

She strolled across the parking lot to the convertible.

"Excuse me," she said. "I didn't mean to eavesdrop, but, well, you guys both talk pretty loudly. Are you a banker?"

"That's right. Now if—"

"Which bank?"

"First Florida Sunshine Savings."

"Oh. Right. I read about you guys."

"I beg your pardon?"

"That article in the *Wall Street Journal*."

"I'm not familiar with any—"

"Riiight." Gloria turned to the other guy. "Good luck, sir. You're going to need it. From what I read, FFSS has a bad CAMEL rating. You know: capital, assets, management, earnings, and liquidity."

"Now, see here, young lady," sputtered the banker.

But Gloria kept on going. "I don't think it's enough to start a run on the bank or, you know, a full-scale liquidity panic—not right away, anyhow—but thank goodness for the FDIC, you know what I mean?"

The passenger looked a little queasy. He was turning green around the gills.

"Then again, Arnold"—Gloria could tell she had the guy on the ropes—"maybe potential insolvency, knowledge-process outsourcing, and balance sheets that don't actually balance aren't the kinds of fiduciary irregularities that make you lose sleep at night. Maybe that's just me. Have a great day."

She waltzed away.

I waltzed after her.

"What was all that stuff you were talking about?"

"More business buzzwords. I'm not even sure what they all mean. But hopefully I said enough of 'em to make that particular vulture buzz off."

And once again, I was seriously happy that Gloria Ortega was on Team Wonderland.

Eggxact Plans

Grandpa knew a lawn-and-garden-supply place that had just what we were looking for.

"Heckerman's has kept my garden gnome collection up to date for over twenty years," he explained. "I already called Izabel Heckerman. She has a giant plastic Easter egg in her warehouse. She said she'd pull it out of storage for us."

"How much is it going to cost to rent it for a day?" I asked, because we had already spent close to two hundred dollars to pick up an Xbox for our grand prize.

"No charge," said Grandpa as we pulled into Heckerman's. "But we have to put a sign on the egg: Courtesy of Heckerman's Garden Center."

"Done," said Gloria.

I didn't disagree. Fact: you don't have to be a

business genius like Gloria to know that free is always a good price.

  We drove back to the Wonderland and stowed the egg and the Xbox in Grandpa's workshop.

We started filling the smaller plastic eggs with smaller prizes and lining them up on Grandpa's workbench.

"So where are you thinking about hiding it?" asked Gloria.

"Maybe inside that municipal garbage can on the beach."

Gloria cocked an eyebrow. "Seriously? A garbage can? What if the garbage truck comes along and dumps it out? Buh-bye, egg. Buh-bye, Xbox."

"The garbage guys always come between six and seven a.m. They're my morning alarm clock. If we do the trash can, we can make this a mapless treasure hunt and just sell clue cards. You know, stuff like 'A surly green puppet calls this hiding place home.'"

"That's an extremely easy clue," said Gloria. "Every kid in America knows Oscar the Grouch lives in a trash can."

"True. But which trash can are we talking about? The one in the lobby? The ones by the pool? The next clue will let you know it's outside. . . ."

"And clue number two costs another five bucks?"

"Yep. We don't give away the beach location till maybe clue six."

"P.T., we cannot charge thirty bucks to find the answer, or only rich kids will be able to play. Do you know any rich kids?"

"No. Not really. Okay. I'll go scout out a better

location and work on the riddles. You work on your dad."

"My dad? Um, why?"

"We need to be on TV again."

"He can't do another report about the Wonderland."

"Why not?"

"Because he already did one. One is all anybody ever gets."

"What do you mean? The president of the United States is on TV almost every day."

"We're not the president. We're a dinosaur egg hunt."

"Dinosaurs are extremely rare," I insisted.

"So are *plastic* dinosaur eggs!"

I guess we were both getting a little cranky. It can be stressful trying to come up with a scheme that will make lightning strike twice. It was hard to guarantee a repeat of our wildly successful pirate treasure hunt.

We decided to step outside and grab some fresh air and maybe come up with some fresher ideas for our riddles.

Near Freddy the Frog, Grandpa was talking to an elderly gentleman with a mustache who looked a lot like that other guy, Bob Jones—the senior citizen who had booked our last room.

"P.T.? Gloria?" Grandpa waved at us to come

over. "You won't believe this. This is Johnny Jones. He's Bob's little brother. And guess what? Sheila—my angel in the red polka-dot scarf—she's their sister!"

37

Family Feud?

With a bigger smile than I'd ever seen on his face before, Grandpa gazed at a faded color photograph of a glamorous woman in mysterious ant-eye sunglasses and a red scarf with white polka dots.

Grandpa held on to the picture like he never wanted to let it go.

"That's Sheila," he said. "Just like I remember her."

"Yeah," said the new Mr. Jones. "She sent me a postcard from here. Just like the one my brother flashed at the camera when he was talking to that reporter on TV. Still have it." He tapped the back pocket of his cargo pants. "I thought, hey, maybe Sheila's over at this Wonderland Motel place, too. Maybe she liked your motel so much back when it was called Wonder World she invited Bob to join her here so they could, you know, catch up on old times. Thought I'd get in on the fun. Figured we could have us a nice little family-reunion-type situation."

I raised my hand. "Um, your brother, Bob, he said Sheila here was his 'lady friend,' not his sister."

I'm not sure, but I think Johnny Jones's left eyeball twitched a little when I said that.

"Sure, sure," the old man said with a nervous chuckle. "That's what Bobby always called Sissy. His 'lady friend.'"

"Isn't that kind of creepy?" said Gloria.

"No," said Johnny Jones. "They both liked that cartoon. You know, *Lady and the Tramp*—the one with the dogs eating spaghetti. Bob just meant Sissy liked spaghetti."

Ew. I was with Gloria. The Jones family was definitely creepy.

"Well," said Grandpa, "I wish I could say your sister was here, Johnny. But she isn't. I haven't seen her since 1973."

"That's too bad," said Mr. Jones. "I ain't seen her since then, neither."

"Seriously?" said Gloria. "You guys don't do Thanksgiving or Christmas together?"

"No," said Mr. Jones, shaking his head. "We have what you might call certain family issues."

"How'd that happen?" I asked, because like Gloria, I was curious about what could be so bad that it tore a family apart for more than four decades.

Mr. Jones fixed me with a stare. It wasn't a very friendly stare, either. In fact, for a split second, it was so fierce his other eyeball started twitching, too. Fact: the old man was extremely twitchy.

Then his mustache started kangarooing. He had an alligator tattoo crawling up the side of his neck, and while his face quivered, the gator's jaws throbbed.

"How do these things always happen?" he said, forcing himself to smile. "My sister and my brother had a big fight. Who remembers what it was about?"

He tugged on his shirt collar to cover up everything but the snarling tattoo's very angry eyes.

"Anyways, after they had their fight, my brother turned on me. Our fight was even worse. We all decided it might be best if we, you know, went our separate ways and didn't see each other for a minimum of thirty years, which became more like forty-five with time added for bad behavior."

"So," I said, "you haven't seen your sister *or* your brother since 1970-something?"

"That's right, kid. Not till I saw him and you on the TV news up in Jacksonville. So, where is he? Where's my big brother, Bob?"

He rudely snatched the photograph out of Grandpa's hands. I say rudely because Grandpa was still gazing at it. He had the same dreamy look in his eyes that Mom has whenever she talks to Mr. Ortega.

"What room, old-timer?" he asked Grandpa.

"I don't really—"

He didn't wait for Grandpa to finish. He turned to me.

"What room, kid?"

"Well," I said, "we really can't give out that information. You see, here at the Wonderland, we try to protect all our guests' privacy."

"They do," added Gloria. "It's like a hotel law."

"Fine," said the new Mr. Jones. "I'll just hang around till I bump into him."

He pulled out a motel room key and started twirling it around his finger. Mom must've just checked him in.

Yep. Our No Vacancy sign was lit again.

Now a Word from Our Sponsors

As much as the new Mr. Jones was skeeving us both out, Gloria and I needed to focus on the dinosaur egg hunt.

"I have an idea," said Gloria.

"Does it involve me getting an alligator tattooed on my neck?"

"No."

"Good."

Gloria held up her hands like she was framing a picture. "Two words, P.T.: corporate sponsorship."

I nodded even though I had absolutely no idea what those two words meant.

"The garden center gave us the big egg in exchange for a little advertising blurb. Other merchants will do the same." Gloria tucked her hands behind her back and paced in front of Dino's plump plastic legs. "So, for the other prizes, the smaller eggs, we don't just fill them with candy and trinkets."

"We don't?"

"No. We put in coupons from local stores—like a free ice-cream cone at Twistee Treat. We ask the IHOP down the block to give away a stack of Rooty Tooty Fresh 'N Fruity pancakes. We hit up the Suncoast Surf Shop for a boogie board. And get this: we charge them all a fee."

"Really?" This wasn't making much sense. "They're giving us a bunch of free stuff and we're charging them to do it?"

"Correct. They become sponsors, P.T. We plaster their names all over the place."

"You mean like all those patches on a NASCAR driver's racing suit?"

"Exactly!"

"We're not going to stick them all over Dino, are we?"

"No," said Gloria. "But we could hang a few signs and banners off the balcony railings. List the sponsors on the back of every clue card. Stuff like that."

"How much do we charge?"

Gloria smiled. "As much as they're willing to pay!"

● ● ●

Our first stop was the Twistee Treat on Gulf Boulevard. What can I say? It was another scorchingly hot day. Twistee Treat was an easy walk, just up the street, serving sixty-six kinds of cold and refreshing ice cream.

The ice-cream shop actually looked like it belonged on the grounds of the Wonderland: the building resembled a gigantic swirl cone.

The manager was a nice man who agreed to, as Gloria put it, "take a meeting" with us. We sat at a circular picnic table and Gloria made her pitch.

"Sir," she said, "how'd you like to get in on something even sweeter than your ice cream? My partner, P. T. Wilkie, and I are offering a limited number of local retailers exclusive access to our next big event. P.T.? Tell him about it."

"Sir, we at the Wonderland Motel have put together a very fun follow-up to our extremely successful and wildly popular Pirate Chest Treasure Quest promotion."

"Oh, right," said the Twistee Treat manager. "I saw you on TV. You're Walt Wilkie's grandson."

I grinned. TV is a marvelous thing. It makes you famous wherever you go.

"That's right. Well, this time—"

"I lost half my business that day."

"Excuse me?"

"Your treasure hunt was such a big deal nobody

wanted to buy any ice cream. Couple of college kids told me you people were selling green ice cream even though it wasn't Saint Patrick's Day. Plus, traffic was backed up all the way to the Corey Causeway. Nobody wanted to drive to St. Pete Beach except your crazed treasure hunters. About thirty of them parked their cars in my lot because yours was jammed full. You're not really planning on doing some kind of crazy stunt like that again, are you?"

I looked to Gloria. She just blinked and smiled.

I'm so steamed I might melt my roof!

"We'll get back to you on that, sir," she said. "Come on, P.T."

The manager at the IHOP asked us to leave the second I told him who I was.

"I saw you on TV! I also saw those college kids tear up the beach! They scared away half my customers!"

There would be no Rooty Tooty Fresh 'N Fruity anything in our dinosaur eggs.

We received the same not-so-warm welcome at all the beach boutiques. Nobody wanted anything to do with us. Our big plans were nothing but big pains in their patooties.

We hiked back to the Wonderland.

And it looked like one of our local retail establishments had called the cops.

Because a police cruiser was parked right in front of the motel office.

Stop in the Name of the Law

The police car was sitting in the spot where you're only supposed to park for five minutes while you check in.

There's even a sign that says so.

I figured the cops might have to give themselves a ticket, unless, of course, they were checking in.

They weren't.

They were walking out.

And Mr. Frumpkes was right behind them.

"There they are," said Mr. Frumpkes, waggling his bony finger at Gloria and me. "Those are the two juvenile delinquents whose lawless antics ruined my mother's quality of life and had a negative environmental impact on our precious beach sand and fragile seashells. The boy's not very good at history, either!"

One of the cops shot Mr. Frumpkes a raised-eyebrows look. I had a feeling he was just about as tired of spending time with Mr. Grumpface as most of his students were.

"You two should head inside and talk to the motel manager," said the other cop, a lady who seemed to really enjoy popping her chewing gum.

"The manager is my mom," I said.

"Good. She'll fill you in."

"On what?" asked Gloria.

"Basically, we need to ask you folks to limit any future promotional activities to your own property."

"That means stay off the beach, Mr. Wilkie!" shouted Mr. Frumpkes.

"No, it doesn't, sir," said the second cop. "The beach is public property. These two can go there anytime they want. Just no more buried pirate chests or treasure hunts."

"How about if we have an Easter egg hunt?" I asked.

"As long as you keep it confined to the grounds of the Wonderland Motel, we won't have a problem," said the first cop.

"And don't invite too many people," said his partner. "Anybody who wants to hunt for your Easter eggs should park here in your parking lot—not up the boulevard at the IHOP or Twistee Treat."

"And not in front of my mother's house!"

added Mr. Frumpkes. "One of those hooligan treasure hunters nearly gave her a heart attack when his parrot started squawking like a pirate! She's so terrified I had to install burglar alarms, motion detectors, and floodlights all around her house. I wanted to add a vat of boiling oil, but Mother wouldn't let me!"

Now both of the police officers were arching their eyebrows at Mr. Frumpkes.

"Thank you, officers," I said.

"We're sorry if we caused any trouble, officers," said Gloria. "But we were just trying to pursue the American dream. To prove that our lives could be richer, better, and fuller if we worked harder, faster, and smarter."

"Ha!" scoffed Mr. Frumpkes. "Good luck with *that*!"

Now the two police officers were squinting at him.

"Did you just make fun of the American dream, Mr. Frumpkes?" asked the gum-popping cop.

"No, I—I—I . . ."

"Kids?" said the other officer. "Go inside. Have a chat with Ms. Wilkie. We need to have a little talk with Mr. Frumpkes."

Gloria and I did as we were told, even though I really wanted to stay in the parking lot with the cops and watch them chew out Mr. Frumpkes. We definitely could've sold tickets to *that*.

Probably could've raised a ton of money, too.

Half the kids at Ponce de León Middle School would've paid double whatever price we asked.

And even though I'd have been the one selling the tickets, *I* would've paid triple.

Cease and Desist

We checked in with Mom.

She told us the same thing the cops had. Except she used the words "cease and desist," because those were the words the cops had used when they talked to her.

"Mr. Frumpkes and his mother complained," she said. "So did a bunch of businesses up and down the boulevard. I think we have to knock off the extra attractions and events, P.T."

"Why?"

"Because that's what 'cease and desist' means," explained Gloria.

"But they said we could do stuff on our own property."

"Ms. Wilkie, how many spare parking spaces do you have?" asked Gloria.

"You mean ones that aren't reserved for our registered guests?"

"Exactly."

"I don't know. Maybe five. Maybe six."

Gloria turned to me. "So the only people who can participate in our dinosaur egg hunt will be your registered guests plus five, maybe six, other carloads of contestants."

"Well," I said, "what about walk-in traffic?"

"This is Florida. When was the last time you saw anybody walking anywhere?"

"You guys?" said Mom. "I appreciate everything the two of you have done. Honestly, I do. Our rooms are fully booked. You've raised an extra twelve thousand dollars. You guys have been great."

"But what about the one hundred thousand dollars we owe the bank?" I asked.

She sighed before she spoke. "Grandpa and I have a plan. You two just keep entertaining our current guests. We'll take care of finding the rest of the money."

Mom tried her best to put on a cheery face, but I could tell she was faking it.

Gloria and I left the lobby feeling defeated.

She headed up to her room to play with her make-believe stock portfolio.

"If my buy-sell strategy holds up," she said, "maybe we can take that twelve thousand dollars we earned and have your grandfather actually invest it for us."

"You mean gamble with it?"

"There would be some risk involved, yes, but the rewards could be astronomical."

"Fine. You go work on that. I want to check in with Grandpa, see if he can do a dinosaur voice. I think our guests are totally bored with Freddy the Frog."

"Okay. Catch up with you later."

"Later."

I headed toward the pool and Grandpa's workshop.

I wanted to find out what his and Mom's big plan was. How did they expect to raise all that money in less than three weeks?

When I reached the pool, the place was deserted. And I could see why.

Johnny and Bob Jones were holding their family reunion poolside, and the only activity seemed to be Yelling at Each Other Very, Very Loudly.

By the way: they weren't calling each other Johnny and Bob, either.

Johnny and Bob,
Stanley and Sid

Once again, it paid to be a semi-invisible kid.

Even though "Johnny" and "Bob" were too busy screaming at each other to even notice me, I hid behind Freddy the Frog. I didn't have to strain to hear what the two old guys were saying. Both Jones brothers were definitely using their "outdoor voices."

"Did you call the cops on me again, Stanley?" snarled the slightly younger one with the neck tattoo, the one who used to be Johnny Jones but was now Sid Something-or-other. "Is that why they were in the front office giving the motel manager the third degree?"

"No, Sid, I didn't call the fuzz. But are you trying to double-cross *me* again?"

"Will you get it through your thick skull, Stanley? I didn't double-cross you the first time. Sheila double-crossed us both."

"Then what are you doing here?"

"I could ask you the same question."

"Go ahead. Ask."

"What are you doing here?"

"Looking for what you and your girlfriend stole from me," said Stanley.

"Hey, you're the one who brought her into the family business," said Sid.

"But then she wanted to grab the loot and run away with you."

The younger brother tugged at his shirt collar. He touched up his hair, which actually might've been a toupee.

"A lot of chicks dug me back in the seventies, Stan. I was what they called a hunk muffin."

"Too bad you lost your looks in the state pen. That where you picked up that gator tat?"

I swallowed hard. *The younger brother spent time in the state penitentiary?* That meant he might be a violent criminal.

"Yeah," said Sid. "Too bad they didn't lock us up in the same prison."

Oh-kay. Stanley had also done time in prison.

I wondered if that was what Sid had meant when he said he and his brother went their separate ways and "didn't see each other for a minimum of thirty years."

"A minimum of thirty years" sounded an awful lot like a jail sentence—one a judge might give for a pretty serious crime.

"So when'd you get out, Stanley?" Sid asked.

"A month ago. How about you?"

"Two weeks."

Sid put his hands on his bony hips. "So why the sudden interest in this Wonderland Motel?"

"Maybe back in the day Sheila sent me a post-card from some place called Walt Wilkie's Wonder World, which, I come to find out by watching TV, is now called the Wonderland Motel. Maybe in this postcard Sheila sent me forty-some years ago, she told me how she was ratting me out to the fuzz so you and her could run off with the ice."

I watch a lot of old gangster movies on cable TV. In those movies, "ice" isn't what motel guests scoop out of our ice machines. It means diamonds!

Brotherly Love?

I was starting to piece together a theory about who these two brothers might actually be.

I needed to do some research, but skeevy Sid and scuzzy Stan might be the answer to all our money worries.

Of course, first we'd have to find their jewels.

The older brother, Stanley, propped his hands on his hips.

"Your turn, little brother. What are *you* doing here?"

"I saw you on TV, shoving that postcard at the cameras. They played that clip up in Jacksonville."

"So?"

"So," said Sid, pulling a folded-over square of cardboard out of his back pocket, "maybe Sheila sent me the exact same postcard from Walt Wilkie's Wonder World."

"Well, ain't that a co-inky-dink," said Stanley.

"My feelings exactly," said Sid.

"So both of us nutted out that this here Wonderland Motel with all the gewgaws was once known as Walt Wilkie's Wonder World—the last place Miss Sheila Bailey visited before the fuzz nabbed her."

"She was eating pancakes, Stanley. At an IHOP. How'd you know where the cops could find her?"

"I didn't. I just gave the goons who hauled me away a tip. Told them that Sheila was the one holding the goody bag from the Miami hotel heist. Every cop in the state was looking for her."

Sid fidgeted with his collar again. "You give them this Sheila information before or after you told them where to find me?"

"Hey, I just did to you like your girlfriend done to me."

"For the last time, she wasn't my girlfriend."

The two brothers weren't yelling so loudly anymore. In fact, they sort of sounded like they were running out of gas. They sounded old.

"I figure we have a decision to make here, Stanley."

"Oh, yeah? What's that, Sidney?"

"We can keep sniping at each other, hashing over the past. Or we can be smart for the first time in a long time. We can let bygones be bygones and bury the hatchet. You and me both think Sheila squirreled away the loot somewheres here on the motel property, on account of what she wrote on the back of our postcards. Am I right?"

"Maybe."

"Well, if we work together, compare notes, maybe we can finally cash in on the hotel heist. Maybe we can finally find our loot!"

Stanley fiddled with his mustache. "Well, we know Sheila ain't coming back for it, may she rest in peace."

"She didn't last a year behind bars," said his little brother.

Then they both chuckled.

"Served her right," said Stanley. "Trying to come between us like that."

"Yeah," said Sidney. "Nobody can break up the Sneemer brothers. Not forever, anyways."

Stanley held out his hand.

Sidney took it.

For the first time in over forty years, the infamous Sneemer brothers were a team again.

Fact: I knew their last name was Sneemer before they said it, because I watch true crime shows on TV.

I also knew that our elderly guests had to be the jewel thieves from the Miami Palm Tree Hotel heist, the guys I'd seen when I was flipping through the channels with Cheeseball.

And they were at the Wonderland, hoping to recover the five million dollars' worth of diamonds and jewelry they had stolen back in 1973.

Because this was where their accomplice hid the goods!

(See? I told you living in a motel is always exciting!)

Total Change of Plans

The brothers finally left the pool.

"You think anybody heard us yakkin'?" asked Sidney as the two old men hobbled away.

"Nah," said Stanley. "Ain't nobody around. They all ran away the first time you said, 'Scram, this could get ugly.'"

"And you said, 'Not as ugly as you!'"

Both brothers laughed again. They even slapped each other on the back.

I clung to the side of Freddy the Frog. Good thing the Sneemer brothers were walking *away* from the waterslide, toward a unit on the first floor.

"You show me your postcard," I heard Stanley say. "I'll show you mine."

"Fine," said Sid. "Two heads are better than one. Two postcards, too."

Finally, their voices faded.

I waited another ten seconds, then bounded up the steps. I needed to talk to Gloria about this.

Okay, I could've talked to Mom or even Grandpa, but I was pretty sure they'd make me do the safe and responsible thing. You know—stay out of it. Call the police. Let the grown-ups handle it.

But the Wilkie family needed those diamonds and jewels even more than the Sneemer brothers did. Sidney and Stanley didn't have a motel with a one-hundred-thousand-dollar balloon loan all set to blow up in their faces.

Of course, I really didn't want the stolen jewels. What I wanted was the reward for *finding* them. At least, I hoped there would still be some kind of a reward.

I hurried down the second-floor terrace to room 233 and knocked on the door.

Gloria opened it.

I must've looked pretty excited, because the first thing she said when she saw me was "What? What's going on?"

"Forget the stock portfolio. Forget the dinosaur egg hunt. There might be five million dollars hidden somewhere on the Wonderland property!"

"This is your new idea?" said Gloria. "To hide a suitcase stuffed with five million dollars somewhere on the motel grounds?"

"No. Those two brothers. The old guys. Johnny and Bob Jones. They're really Sid and Stanley Sneemer. And I'm ninety-nine percent sure they're also notorious jewel thieves."

"And you think this because . . . ?"

"They were down at the pool talking about the ice they stole."

"Maybe they filled their whole coolers with ice from the machine. That's against posted motel rules. You're only supposed to take enough to fill a bucket."

I shook my head. "'Ice' is gangster-speak for 'diamonds.'"

"Really?" This time, Gloria rolled her eyes to the right, like she wanted someone else (even though there was nobody there) to see what a nutjob I was. "I think you're taking this whole 'marvels to behold and stories to be told' thing a little too far, P.T. Seriously. Diamonds?"

"This is the truth. I'm just giving you cold, hard facts. Go on. Google them." I gestured toward her open laptop. "I saw a true crime TV show about what those two did back in the seventies."

Gloria hovered her fingers over the keyboard.

"Who am I looking for again? Stanley Steemer?"

"No, not Stanley Steemer! The Sneemer brothers. Sid and Stanley. Jewel thieves. Miami hotel heist. In 1970-something."

She typed in the search information.

Google took, like, half a second to show her half a million results.

"Wow," was all Gloria said. "Okay. I take back all my snarky remarks. You're actually right."

"I knew it!"

Gloria read chunks of a Web page out loud. "'Sidney and Stanley Sneemer burglarized the posh Miami Palm Tree Hotel in June 1973. They stole approximately five million dollars' worth of diamond-, emerald-, and ruby-encrusted jewelry from the motel safe.'"

Gloria stopped reading.

"That was five million dollars in 1973," she said.

"How much would that be worth today?"

Gloria twiddled her fingers in the air like she was using a calculator. "Approximately twenty-seven million."

We both whistled.

Then Gloria went back to the Web page.

"'Stanley Sneemer, the older brother and brains of the operation, was arrested two weeks after the burglary, thanks to a tip police received from an anonymous caller.'"

"Sheila Bailey," I said. "Grandpa's angel with the red polka-dot scarf. She was the one who told the police about Stanley."

"Seriously?"

"Yep. I think Sheila was crushing on his little brother, Sid. Apparently, 'chicks dug' him."

Gloria tapped her laptop screen. "Must be why hours after Stanley was arrested, he gave up his younger brother, Sidney, to the police. And he told them about Sid's accomplice, a 'beautiful blond bombshell' named Sheila 'Boom-Boom' Bailey."

"Boom-Boom? Grandpa's angel had a middle name and it was Boom-Boom?"

"Yep." Gloria read more details. "Stanley Sneemer gave the cops a picture of Ms. Bailey, who was 'on the lam' and lying low."

"She was hiding right here," I said. "At Walt Wilkie's Wonder World. She stayed here for nearly a week and sent postcards to both of the brothers. Then somebody must've spotted her."

Gloria nodded. "It says two police officers were sipping coffee at the International House of Pancakes on Gulf Boulevard when Sheila Bailey walked in and ordered a stack of flapjacks for supper."

"Sheila was the one who actually had the jewels," I said. "The brothers think she brought the loot here and hid it somewhere on the grounds."

"Well, if she did, she never told the police or the Amalgamated Insurance Company, which offered a reward of one hundred and fifty thousand dollars for 'any information leading to the safe return of the stolen jewels.' It says she told the police she'd 'just blown into St. Pete that morning.'"

"The cops didn't know she'd been staying at Walt Wilkie's Wonder World for, like, a week?"

"Nope. Not according to this old news story."

"So," I said, "that means nobody's ever searched the motel grounds."

Gloria kept reading off her computer screen.

"'Sheila Bailey was charged as an accomplice, sent to prison, and, ten months later, died in her cell, taking any secrets about where she might have hidden the stolen jewelry to the grave with her.'"

"So now the two brothers are finally out of jail," I said. "They want to search our property for the stolen jewels because they both have postcards Sheila sent them from Walt Wilkie's Wonder World, a place that technically doesn't exist anymore."

"But then you flashed that old postcard on TV. You gave them the exact address!"

Yep. I did. Just like Gloria told me to.

Money Is Its Own Reward

We called a number we found for the Amalgamated Insurance Company down in Miami.

"Yes," said a very helpful customer service repre-
sentative after we listened to hold music (extremely
annoying violins) for nearly fifteen minutes, "that
one-hundred-and-fifty-thousand-dollar reward is still
being offered. Do you have information you would
like to share with Big Irv Investigators?"

"Who?" I asked.

"Big Irv Investigators," replied the telephone
lady. We had her on speaker so Gloria and I could
both hear her. "It is the private detective firm that
has recently taken over the investigation into the
Miami Palm Tree Hotel burglary case for Amalgamated Insurance."

"Do, uh, we get the reward if we tell Big Irv what we think we know?"

"Yes, you will receive a percentage of Big Irv's payout if your information helps him locate the missing jewels. However, you sound like children. . . ."

"Is that a problem?" I asked. "Doesn't Big Irv give rewards to kids?"

"Well, yes. He has told us any informants would, as I stated, receive a percentage of what Big Irv earns from Amalgamated."

Gloria leaned in closer to the phone. "How much?" she asked.

"It is my understanding that Big Irv is offering up to one percent for information that leads to his finding the stolen items."

Gloria made a stinky face. "Up to one percent?"

"That is correct."

"So this Big Irv would give us fifteen hundred dollars from his one hundred and fifty thousand—or maybe less—even if we're the ones who crack the case?"

"I'm sorry. I don't have any more specific information. Might I suggest you contact Big Irv Investigators in Boca Raton?"

"Thanks," I said. "We'll do that."

Gloria was shaking her head and mouthing, "No, we will not do that."

"And," I asked the phone, "if we find the missing jewelry all by ourselves, do we just call you guys again to collect our one hundred and fifty thousand dollars?"

"Yes. However, it is my duty to inform you that trying to recover stolen goods on your own, without the assistance of adults and expert professionals, could prove dangerous and potentially lethal."

"Right," I said. "Thanks for the heads-up."

I hung up the phone.

"'Lethal' means deadly, right?" I asked Gloria.

"Correct."

"Right. Just thought I'd double-check that."

If we could find the jewels, we could pay off the loan and have fifty thousand dollars left over. Mom could square things with the bank and we'd all live happily ever after—if, of course, our detective work didn't turn out to be lethal.

"You ready to do some snooping?" I asked Gloria.

"Sure. What've we got to lose? I mean, besides our lives?"

● ● ●

The rest of the day, we pretended like we were still setting up the dinosaur egg hunt on the motel grounds.

That gave us an excuse to slink around the

property, hide behind shrubberies, and, basically, tail Sid and Stanley Sneemer while they went on a walking tour of the Wonderland grounds. Both brothers were wearing baseball caps, probably to shield their eyes and shadow their faces.

They came to the big Muffler Man statue.

"We need to open him up," said Stanley. "Take a peek inside."

"I got a hacksaw and a drill."

"Good. We do it after dark. Two or three in

the morning. When all these tourists and collegiate types are asleep."

"Sounds like a plan," said Sid. "You hungry?"

"Yeah. Stack of pancakes would sure hit the spot."

Both brothers laughed again.

"Sheila's last supper," said Sid.

"Let's head over to that IHOP where the cops grabbed her," said Stanley. "It seems like the perfect thing to do."

"Poetic justice," added Sidney.

The Sneemer brothers snickered some more and drifted out of the parking lot.

"We need to see their postcards," I whispered to Gloria. "From what they were saying out by the pool, there's some kind of clue on them."

"Well, where are these postcards?"

"Not sure. But their rooms would be a good place to start looking. We should do it right now—while they're off eating dinner."

"Um, isn't it against the law to enter motel rooms without a guest's permission?"

"Only if they're not jewel thieves."

"Oh. Okay. But how, exactly, are we going to get into their rooms?"

I grinned. "Don't worry. I know people with a master key to every single door in the motel!"

The Key to Success

Clara has been a housekeeper at the Wonderland Motel for as long as I can remember.

She was just finishing her shift when I caught up with her on the first floor, near the laundry room.

Gloria had gone to the lobby to find out what rooms the "Jones" brothers were staying in. (I told her to tell Mom that the two brothers had both won extreme shuffleboard, a game we'd invented using grapefruits instead of shuffle pucks, and we needed to deliver their prizes to their rooms.)

"Clara!" I said, panting hard, like I'd been running all over searching for her. "There you are!"

She looked me up and down.

"We have an emergency in one of the rooms!"

Clara simply arched an eyebrow. She doesn't panic easily.

"*¿Otro inodoro obstruido?*"

"Yes," I said, building on what Clara had just given me, "another clogged toilet!"

Fact: when you live in a motel, you learn how to say "clogged toilet" in several different languages.

I remember, once, a college boy tried to flush a whole watermelon down the toilet because it was made of water and would dissolve. What do they teach this boy at his college? Many college boys are book smart but toilet dumb.

"Do you know how many clogged toilets I have plunged in my years of service to your family, Señor P.T.?"

"Too many!"

"Eh?"

"Mom and I were both just saying it isn't fair that you're always the one who has to unclog all the, you know, *inodoros obstruidos*."

"Only for two more years," said Clara. "Then my daughter, she graduate medical school. University Florida. Go, Gators."

"Clara," I said, "Mom and I want to make absolutely certain that you're one hundred percent happy in your position here at the Wonderland Motel."

"Oh, I am, P.T. *Muy, muy feliz*. You know how much I love *tu madre* and *tu abuelo* and you."

She reached for the plunger.

"Let me do it."

"No, P.T. It is my job."

"But your shift is over. If you lend me your plunger and a passkey, I'll go take care of the, uh, mess myself."

I held out my hand.

"*¿Estás seguro?*"

"Yes, Clara. I'm sure."

"*Gracias.*"

She slid the master key off her key ring and handed it to me.

· 188 ·

"You are a very sweet boy. I hope it isn't another college boy with a watermelon."

"Me too. Oh, can I borrow your clipboard?"

"My clipboard?"

"I like to keep notes when I unclog toilets."

Up went that skeptical eyebrow. "You do?"

"Sure. If we keep records and figure out which rooms are clogging their toilets on a regular basis, we can cut back on the number of toilet paper rolls we put in those bathrooms while keeping an eye out for any incoming watermelons."

Clara arched her eyebrow even higher.

"It was, uh, Grandpa's idea," I sputtered.

"*Sí, sí.*" She shook her head. "Señor Grandpa."

Then she tweeted like a cuckoo bird.

Like I said, Clara has worked at the Wonderland since forever. She is very used to Grandpa and his nutty ideas.

She handed me her clipboard. It had a list of all the rooms in the motel. She checked them off as she cleaned them. I've always found that carrying a clipboard makes you look more official and authorized.

Even when what you're really doing is sneaking into somebody's room.

Postcards from the Past

I ran to the lobby just as Gloria was coming out.

"Rooms 103 and 114," she said.

"Room 103 is closer," I said. "We'll start there."

We went to the door and knocked.

"Housekeeping," I announced, pretending to check Clara's clipboard, just in case any other guests were watching us.

No answer.

I knocked again.

"Housekeeping."

Still no response.

"Whose room is this?" I asked.

"Bob Jones," said Gloria. "So that means he's, uh . . ."

"Stanley. The older brother."

I slid the key into the lock.

"Don't turn on the lights," I told Gloria. "Just in case they finish dinner early. We don't want them knowing somebody's in here."

We tiptoed around the room, both of us using our smartphones as flashlights.

"Bingo," said Gloria.

"You found it?"

"Yep."

"What's it say?"

"'Welcome to Walt Wilkie's Wonder World.'"

"I meant on the back."

"Oh. Right." She flipped it over. "Ew. Gross. Some lady kissed the stamp with her grungy red lipstick."

"Yeah," I said. "I saw that when Stanley—I mean, 'Bob Jones'—checked in. Seriously disgusting."

"Okay, it says, 'Stanley—you think you're such a big, big man. Always smiling! Ha! If you ask me, you're all empty inside. Too bad you'll never take that trip to Happy Town you've been planning, because I'm hiding the rocks someplace you'll never find them. P.S. I'm calling the cops on you. You'll be in jail long before you figure out the clue I just gave you. P.P.S. I dig Sid. Your little brother is a hunk muffin.'"

Roadkill

Gloria and I didn't need to be Nancy Drew and Sherlock Holmes to figure out why the Sneemer brothers were eyeballing Smilin' Sam, the Wonderland's big, empty-inside man.

"You think Sheila Bailey really hid the diamonds inside the Muffler Man statue?" asked Gloria.

"Maybe," I said. "He's a 'big, big man.' He's hollow—so he's definitely 'empty inside.' He's always smiling, because he's molded that way. Sheila might've found or cut a tiny hole in the statue so she could slip the bag of jewels inside."

"That's probably what the Sneemer brothers think," said Gloria. "Maybe that's why they decided to go to dinner right after they checked out Smilin' Sam. Maybe they saw a patched-over hole!"

"We should check it out, too—right after we check out that other postcard."

"Why do we need the other one?" asked Gloria.

"Because Sheila probably sent an even better clue to Sid. Don't forget, back in 1973, she had a crush on the guy."

"Right. He was a 'hunk muffin.'"

"Besides, this might be our only chance to search his room, too. Who knows when they'll leave the motel grounds again? Come on."

"P.T.?"

"Yeah?"

"I still think searching someone's room without permission or, you know, a search warrant is totally illegal."

"Maybe it is. And I promise I'll look it up if I ever become a cop or a lawyer. For now, I'm just a kid trying to save his family and their motel. Plus, I have a clipboard, so we look official."

"Okay," said Gloria. "I can live with that. Let's book."

We locked up Stanley's room and hurried down to 114. Once again, Clara's passkey did the trick.

"Gross," said Gloria.

"Totally."

The room was dark except for a table lamp Sid had left on. The lamp was right next to his hairpiece, which looked like a squirrel after a truck rolls over it on the freeway.

And the postcard was tucked under the toupee.

"I'm not touching anything near that flattened hair mat," said Gloria.

"I've got it," I said.

I used one of the Wonderland pens next to the message pad on the bedside table to pry up the trampled carpet of fake hair. Carefully sliding the postcard out from under what looked like roadkill, I tried to breathe through my mouth, because the limp toupee smelled like Vicks VapoRub mixed with masking tape glue.

The front of the Wonder World postcard was exactly the same as the one we'd found in Stanley Sneemer's room. The note on the back, of course, was way different. Plus, Sheila had dotted all the *i*'s on Sid's card with hearts.

I read her message out loud: "'Sid, Schnookums. With your blowhard brother out of the picture, the two of us can book a one-way ticket to Happy Town—if you're not afraid of hurting the big, empty-headed man. Follow my tracks. See you soon, hunk muffin. P.S. I just gave you a clue, cutie. P.P.S. I know which rock I want on my engagement ring. The biggest one.'"

"Okay," said Gloria. "She's definitely talking diamonds."

"And 'hurting the big, empty-headed man' means cutting into Smilin' Sam!"

We slapped each other a high five, something I only do when I am extremely pumped.

This was huge. We'd cracked the case. All that reward money would be ours! The Wonderland was saved!

That's when I heard a key slide into the door lock.

The Sneemer brothers were back!

Thinking Fast

I quickly slipped the postcard back under the bad wig. I plucked up the clipboard.

Fluorescent fixtures flickered on all around us.

"What the—" said Sid, who'd just flipped up the light switch next to the door.

"What are you two kids doing in my brother's room?" demanded Stanley.

Gloria looked a little like Bambi caught in a locomotive's headlight.

I smiled. Ticked a box on my clipboard.

"We were just checking your minibar, sir."

"What?"

"We wanted to make sure you had all the soda pop, Pringles, and M&M'S you needed in your fridge. Are you interested in some extra Dr. Brown's sodas? Might I suggest Cel-Ray or black cherry?"

"This room doesn't have a fridge!" said Sid.

"Huh," I said with a dumb nod. "No wonder we couldn't find it."

"It might've helped if you turned on the lights."

"Good point, Mr. Jones." I scribbled on my clipboard. "We'll make a note of that. Turn . . . on . . . lights. . . ."

"You're the kid what was on TV, right?" said Stanley.

"Yes, sir. P. T. Wilkie. My mother is the manager of this motel, and, well, frankly, we're a little short-staffed right now. Jimmy Joe Bob, the guy who usually restocks the minibars, took the week off. Mom handed me his clipboard and asked me to fill in. Gloria here is auditioning to become my summer intern."

"That means if I land the job, I won't get paid," said Gloria.

"I told you kids," said Sid, "this room ain't got no minibar!"

"I guess that's why they say, 'You learn something new every day.' For instance, did you know that my grandfather called this place Walt Wilkie's Wonder World back in the 1970s?"

"Yeah," said Stanley. "We've seen the postcards. Our sister stayed here."

"Right," I said. "I remember you mentioning that."

Suddenly, I got an idea.

"Her name was Sheila, right?"

"What's it to you, kid?"

"Well, did Grandpa tell you about the map she gave him?"

"Map?"

Yep. I was already cooking up a new scheme.

"That's right. A map. Grandpa forgot all about it until he talked to you, Mr. Jones. But then, just seeing that photo of your sister triggered a memory. Right before she left and never came back, your sister, Sheila, gave my grandfather some kind of map thingy."

The two brothers looked at each other. I think they were thinking what I hoped they'd be thinking.

"'Follow my tracks,'" mumbled Sid, obviously recalling that phrase from the back of his postcard.

"The map might be our ticket to Happy Town," Stanley muttered in reply.

"What are you guys talking about?" I asked.

"Nothin', kid," snapped Sid. "Nothin'."

"So, where is this here map?" asked Stanley, hiking up his baggy pants like the tough guy he used to be, even though his belt was already above his belly button.

"I'm keeping the map safe in my room," I told them. "Grandpa gave it to me because I think it's such a neat souvenir from 1973. I thought I'd take it to school for show-and-tell on Monday, because we're studying 1973 in class and—"

Sid started shaking his head. "You're not taking our sister's map to no school, kid. You're giving it to us."

Stanley hiked up his pants even higher and made the most threatening look he could still make. "And you're doing it right now!"

Treasure Hunt II

"Sir, you are correct," I said.

"I know I am," said Sidney.

"Your sister drew the map, so it definitely belongs to you guys. Those have been the map rules since way back in pirate days. If one pirate drew a map to the spot where, let's say, he had buried his treasure, and then, let's also say, he caught a cannonball in the belly and croaked, then the map would go to his next of kin."

"I read about that, too," said Gloria, trying to help me out. "It was in this pirate almanac they had in the school library and—"

"Just fork over the map," snarled Stanley.

"I have to go get it first," I said.

"Then go!" said Sid. "And bring it back. Chop-chop."

I shot him a jolly thumbs-up. "You've got it, sir. Back in a flash."

Gloria and I bolted out the door.

"That was close," said Gloria.

"Yeah. But it was also exciting."

"Exciting? Those two are convicted felons, P.T. Plus, they were given extra prison time for bad behavior. I think they might have anger-management issues."

"Yeah. That's what I'm kind of counting on."

"Huh?"

"It's all part of my master plan."

"Really? You have a plan?"

"Every story has a plan, Gloria. You have to sort of know where you're going before you start, or you'll never make it to the end."

"So what exactly are you going to give those two thugs? Their so-called sister, Sheila, didn't really leave your grandfather a treasure map, or we would've been using it to find the jewels, correct?"

"Yep. I'm going to give them the second map we used the other day for our Pirate Chest Treasure Quest. The old-fashioned parchment paper makes it look kind of old, like it's been around since 1973."

"Um, P.T.?" said Gloria. "That map will take them from the swimming pool to the fence behind

Mrs. Frumpkes's house. Mr. Frumpkes doesn't want people digging up his mother's 'backyard,' remember?"

"Of course I do."

"He put in all those alarms and security lights. If those two old coots start digging up Mrs. Frumpkes's sand, Mr. Frumpkes will call the cops on them."

I was grinning from ear to ear. "Exactly!"

● ● ●

I delivered a copy of our second treasure-hunt map to Sidney's room (after crumpling it into a ball, uncrumpling it, stomping on it in the sand, spilling some iced tea on it, and generally trying to "age" it).

"Thanks, kid," said Sidney. "Now scram!"

"Yes, sir," I said. I even saluted.

Gloria was waiting for me outside the room. We put our ears against the closed door so we could eavesdrop.

"We should check out the big smiling-man statue first," said Stanley.

"Nah," said Sidney. "This map is more Sheila's style. She was sort of a freaky-deaky doofus. Spent too much time disco dancing. The mirror ball messed with her mind, you know what I mean, man?"

"Fine," we heard Stanley say. "We weren't going to cut open the big bozo till two or three in the morning anyways. If this map don't pan out, we'll come back and slice open the giant galoot."

They'd taken the bait.

Gloria and I raced back to our rooms and changed into our best spy clothes. You know: black on black on black. The sun had set, and we wanted to disappear into the darkness while we tailed the Sneemer brothers.

"Tell me again why we're doing this?" whispered Gloria as we hid behind a palm tree.

"To make sure Mr. Frumpkes takes them off the game board."

"Why don't we just go check out the Smilin' Sam statue while they're off on their wild-goose chase?"

"Because we don't want them coming back before we're done and catching us cutting open the holes they want to cut open. Like you said, they have those anger-management issues. Who knows? They might also have guns."

The two brothers were talking loudly in the distance. They seemed like the kind of stubborn old people who refuse to wear hearing aids even though they know they need them.

"This is crazy, Sid," Stanley yelled at his brother. "If Sheila buried the jewels right here on the beach, some yahoo with a metal detector

probably found them years ago. A lot of them diamonds and rubies were on gold rings."

"Then how come we ain't never read about anybody digging up our loot?" said Sid. "We're talking
five million dollars' worth of ice and rocks. That
woulda made the news."

The two brothers followed the map, made all the
correct turns, shuffled across the sand, and, finally,
reached the fence behind Mrs. Frumpkes's house.

Leaning against the railings for support, the two creaky crooks hunkered down and started shoveling with their hands like dogs with a bone they needed to bury in a hurry.

Sand went flying everywhere. In fact, Sid and Stanley were kicking up such a dust storm it triggered the newly installed motion detectors mounted to Mrs. Frumpkes's back fence.

Bright halogen floodlights thumped on, accompanied by a twirling red light, a *whoop-whoop*ing siren, and a computerized voice that kept repeating, "Intruder alert. Intruder alert."

"Stop!" whined a nasal voice. "Cease and desist. The police have been summoned."

It was Mr. Frumpkes. He was shining a ginormous flashlight at the Sneemer brothers, who instinctively raised their hands high over their heads.

"The cops?" Sidney turned to his brother. "You set me up? Again? You lousy chump!"

"Who you calling a chump, chump?"

The two old men started whaling on each other.

Fists pounded into ribs.

Legs kicked at the sand and shins.

The Sneemer brothers tumbled down the beach, using all sorts of words I probably shouldn't repeat.

That's when we heard another siren.

A police car, with its light bar flashing, screeched to a stop in the driveway at Mrs. Frumpkes's house.

Sidney and Stanley Sneemer kept fighting as hard as two out-of-shape, ancient ex-cons can.

A pair of police officers burst onto the beach.

It only took them a couple of minutes to pry Stanley and Sidney apart. They slapped them in handcuffs and led them around the fence to their cop car.

The Sneemers were going to spend the night in jail.

That meant Gloria and I officially had first dibs on Smilin' Sam!

Sam the Man

We raced back to the Wonderland.

"This is our chance," I said to Gloria. "We can cut the Muffler Man open while the Sneemer brothers spend the night in jail!"

"What cuts through fiberglass?"

"A drill, maybe. Or a jigsaw. Grandpa has a bunch of power tools in his workshop."

It was nearly midnight. Most of the motel was dark, except for the neon sign out front. Its glowing No Vacancy tubes were throbbing green.

We made our way into Grandpa's workshop. I could hear him snore-whistle-snoring up in his sleeping loft. I quietly grabbed a cordless drill with a one-inch-wide bit, a jigsaw with a jagged blade, a hammer, and a crowbar.

I figured one of them ought to do the job.

We tiptoed out of the workshop and crept to the Smilin' Sam statue. Fortunately, Mom goes to sleep every night at eleven—usually at her desk . . . over a pile of bills. Gloria tells me Mr. Ortega goes to bed even earlier, because he has to get up at five o'clock on a regular basis to do that morning newscast.

Gloria crouched down and examined every inch of the giant statue's boots and legs. "I don't see anything that looks like a patched-over hole. This may not be where Sheila hid the jewels."

"It has to be!" I said.

"Why?"

"Because this story needs a happy ending."

"Um, P.T., you can't just make up stuff and have life magically turn out the way you want it to."

"I can try!"

I powered on the whirring drill. It whined worse than the one at the dentist.

"Can you also try to keep quiet?"

"Sorry. This drill doesn't have a silencer."

"Well, work fast! Start with the boots."

"Why?"

"Because if Sheila 'Boom-Boom' Bailey was planning a grab-and-go, she wouldn't hide them too high."

"Good point. I'll drill a hole in the heel of his left boot. Once I do, I can slip in the jigsaw blade

·208·

and slice out a circle of plastic big enough for us to poke a head through."

Fact: no kid should ever try anything this crazy at home without adult supervision—unless, of course, they have a motel to save.

It felt like we were doing shoe repair on an overgrown action figure. The blade kept bouncing around, thumping loudly. Finally, after my sweaty shirt was coated with chunky white sawdust, I punched out a huge slab of fiberglass from the back of Smilin' Sam's left work boot.

I flipped on my smartphone flashlight app and stuck my head inside. I searched the bottom first.

"See anything?" asked Gloria, her voice sounding muffled through the quarter-inch-thick molded walls.

"No," I answered. My voice echoed like crazy inside the statue. "I'm going to twist around, check out his shin and stuff. When Sheila hid the jewels, she might've taped them to the interior walls."

"You think the tape would stay stuck after all these years?"

"Maybe. I'm not sure. But if I don't find anything on the inside of this leg, I'll drill into the other boot. If we come up empty again, we'll grab a ladder and cut open his butt and—"

"Oh, no you won't, young man," said a voice on the other side of the fiberglass that didn't sound at all like Gloria's.

Because it belonged to my mother.

Oops

I popped my head out of the boot hole.

"Hi, Mom. Beautiful night, huh?"

My mother was sort of scowling at me. I tried to swipe all the white speckles off my shirt. No luck. They were sweat-glued in place.

"P.T., what exactly are you doing?"

I held up my drill. "Digging for buried treasure!"

"Inside Smilin' Sam?"

"Exactly! You see, Gloria and I have reason to suspect that a team of notorious jewel thieves stashed the loot they stole in the infamous Miami Palm Tree Hotel heist right here inside this very statue. You ever hear of the Miami Palm Tree Hotel?"

My mother shook her head and closed her eyes—the way she does when she's disappointed in me or something I've done.

"Oh, it was quite the swinging hot spot," I said, pouring on the razzle-dazzle. "Swanky. Sophisticated. Posh. Nobody but rich and famous people could afford to stay there. And, as you might imagine, they all wore jewelry!"

Mom stared at me like I was an alien.

"Anyway, the Sneemer brothers," I said as fast as I could, "also known as Bob and Johnny Jones, and their mutual girlfriend, Sheila 'Boom-Boom' Bailey . . ."

"'Boom-Boom'?" said Mom.

"She was Grandpa's blond angel! Anyway, Sheila hid the diamonds and emeralds the Sneemer brothers stole from the hotel safe inside this statue. She said so in two postcards she sent to the brothers from Walt Wilkie's Wonder World! I've seen the postcards!"

"P.T.? Is this another one of your stories?"

"No, Mom. Gloria and I just saved the motel! There's a ginormous one-hundred-and-fifty-thousand-dollar reward for whoever finds the stolen jewelry. That's more money than we need to pay off the balloon loan. Our troubles are over! This is the truth. I swear."

Mom shook her head again. "The truth? You spend so much time in your make-believe worlds I wonder if you even know what the truth is anymore."

Wow.

Not at all what I was going for. I was hoping for more of a "you're my hero" type of vibe.

"What's with all the drilling and hacking and sawing?" Grandpa, in his plaid bathrobe, joined us at the base of Smilin' Sam. "Oh, no. What happened here?"

He'd just seen the gaping hole I'd cut into the back of the boot.

"His feet were sweaty and they needed to breathe a little?" Yes, I was trying to joke my way out of this mess. But no one was laughing. Not even me.

"Ms. Wilkie?" said Gloria. "Mr. Wilkie? P.T. and I were following up on a very reliable tip that suggested we would, indeed, find five million dollars' worth of jewelry—stolen from the vaults of the Miami Palm Tree Hotel in 1973—hidden here inside this large, hollow Muffler Man."

"Nineteen seventy-three?" said Grandpa. He dusted away the fiberglass sawdust that had showered onto the statue's base. "Smilin' Sam didn't join us till *1976.*"

With the base dusted off, I could see a small plaque: "Installed 1976."

In other words, three years *after* Sheila Bailey had been a guest at Walt Wilkie's Wonder World.

"Hey, knock it off down there," someone shouted from the second floor. "We're trying to sleep!"

"Sorry," said Grandpa with a weak wave.

Maybe I'd gotten everything totally wrong. Maybe Sheila had never even hidden the jewels on our property. Maybe she'd stashed them in a locker at the St. Pete bus station. Maybe she'd buried them under a stack of pancakes at the IHOP.

Fact: that thing they say about looking before you leap? It also applies to cutting open fiberglass statuary.

"Sam was a big part of our bicentennial

celebration," Grandpa continued, sounding wistful. "Disney World had their America on Parade celebration for the country's two hundredth birthday. Dozens of floats. Hundreds of character performers. The whole thing lasted half an hour. Me? I had Smilin' Sam. I put a giant Betsy Ross–style flag in his hands. Your grandmother, may she rest in peace, made him an Uncle Sam hat out of cardboard boxes. When it rained, she made him another one. Together, we painted Sam up with stars and stripes. Then we propped a battery-powered cassette deck behind him on his pedestal. It played a loop of fife-and-drum music. Very patriotic. Sometimes, at night, we lit sparklers."

Grandpa's eyes were misty.

"Millions of people watched that big bicentennial parade over at Disney World. A couple dozen took snapshots here with Sam."

"And," said Mom, "we were going to sell this statue to a used-car dealer up in New Jersey."

Suddenly, my mouth was super dry. "You were?"

"Yes. Look, you guys have been a huge help, but to pay off the loan, we need to raise money every way we can. Even if it means selling off a few of our favorite things."

Gloria nodded. "Prudent move. Liquidate assets to stabilize cash flow and build up monetary reserves. How much were you offered for Smilin' Sam?"

"One thousand dollars," said Mom with her saddest sigh yet. "Now we'll be lucky if we get one hundred for it."

"That's our big plan, kiddos," said Grandpa. "Sell off the statues and knickknacks. Raise enough cash to pay off that balloon loan."

"I'm so sorry," I said.

"So am I," said Mom. "Good night, everybody." She walked away.

I turned to Grandpa.

He was already shuffling back to his workshop bedroom. "Tomorrow's another day," he said without his usual zip. "Let's just hope it's better than today."

"I should head upstairs," said Gloria. "My dad

might be wondering where I am. I'll catch up with you tomorrow, P.T."

Watching her slump away, I could tell Gloria was feeling pretty low, too.

But here's another fact: I felt worse than anybody.

B.I. the P.I.

The next morning, I was still feeling miserable.

Mom didn't even talk to me when we split our grapefruit for breakfast. We both just sat there, silently squirting ourselves in the eye.

Then things got worse.

Somebody bopped the bell out in the lobby. Mom stood up like a zombie and trudged out of our kitchenette. She didn't sigh or mutter anything about having to be the only grown-up at the motel. She just said, "Coming."

Since our unit was right off the lobby, I could hear what was going on out there, because Zombie Mom left the door open.

"May I help you, sir?" she asked.

"I surely hope so," boomed a big, jolly voice. "My name is Big Irv. I am a private investigator. My friends call me B.I. the P.I." He chuckled. "Eh, heh, heh, heh."

Mom didn't chuckle back.

"That's nice," she said in a monotone.

You should meet my little brother Ginormous George.

"Ma'am, I am currently working for the Amalgamated Insurance Company down in Miami."

"And what brings you up to St. Petersburg?"

"I'm looking for these two gentlemen. Stanley and Sidney Sneemer. A waitress over at the IHOP told me they might be staying here at the Wonderland."

I more or less leapt up from the table and dashed out to the lobby.

"You mean Bob and Johnny Jones?" said Mom. She was looking at the photographs Big Irv had just shoved across the counter at her.

I, on the other hand, was looking at Big Irv. His name fit. The guy was a giant. A big bear in a business suit. He was so tall it was amazing that he could reach to comb his hair.

"You're the guy investigating the 1973 jewel heist at the Miami Palm Tree Hotel!" I blurted out without thinking (another of my many amazing talents).

"That's right," said Big Irv. "What do you know about that, little man?"

I thought fast. Okay, I just thought. But that was a major improvement over blurting.

"Nothing," I said. "Just, you know, what I've seen on TV. Is there still a one-hundred-and-fifty-thousand-dollar reward for whoever finds the missing jewels? I mean, the burglary took place over forty years ago."

"Doesn't matter," said Big Irv. "The insurance

company is still interested in recovering the stolen goods and recouping their losses. Why do you think I'm up here looking for these two old jailbirds?"

Mom had one eyebrow up quizzically. I think her face was trying to say, *Were you actually telling me the truth last night, P.T.?*

"Wait a second," she said to Big Irv. "The Jones brothers are jailbirds?"

"'Jones' is just an alias they use, ma'am. Sidney and Stanley Sneemer are violent and dangerous felons. They might even be psychotic. They both kept getting extra time added to their prison terms because they didn't play well with others while incarcerated. Then, after forty-some years, they're both finally released—from separate prisons, mind you—for a burglary they committed way back in 1973. A burglary for which the stolen items have never been recovered. And where's the first place they both go when they get out of jail?" He tapped the counter with his wedding ring. "Here. The Wonderland Motel on St. Pete Beach. I see this activity and I have to ask myself one question: Why?"

"Well, we have some very nice amenities," I offered. "For instance, there's free doughnuts and coffee every morning."

"I'm sure you folks run a mighty fine motel, little man. But I have a hunch that the Sneemer brothers didn't come here for the doughnuts or the coffee. I think way back in 1973 their lady friend, Sheila Bailey, stashed their loot somewhere here on the grounds."

"That's what P.T. thought!"

Yep. Mom sometimes blurts without thinking, too.

"I did see the two old guys eyeballing Smilin' Sam. I guess it's possible Sheila Bailey could've stashed the loot inside one of his boots!" I said.

Big Irv put his hands on his hips and glared at me, Frumpkes-style, but with a twinkle in his eye. "And who, exactly, is this Smilin' Sam, little man?"

Let's Make a Deal

"Smilin' Sam is one of our oversized decorative pieces," explained Mom. "Well, it used to be one of ours. It's about to belong to the Roadside Americana Auction Company. They've found it a new home in a used-car dealer's parking lot."

"Did you get a good price?" I asked Mom.

"Better than I thought we would with the damage. Five hundred dollars."

"I'm sorry."

Mom actually smiled. "I'll take the difference out of your allowance."

"Um, I don't actually get an allowance."

Big Irv cleared his throat. "Don't mean to interrupt whatever it is you two are talking about . . ."

"Family stuff," I said. "But you want to talk about that other family, the Sneemer brothers, and where Sheila 'Boom-Boom' Bailey stashed their loot, am I right?"

All of a sudden, I sounded like a tough guy in one of those black-and-white gangster movies Grandpa and I sometimes watch on rainy Saturday afternoons. That was why Mom was now arching her other eyebrow at me.

"Eh, heh, heh, heh," chuckled Big Irv. "What do you know about all that, little man?"

"Nothing, really."

"But you think Sheila stashed the stolen jewelry in this Smilin' Sam statue?"

"I didn't actually say that."

Big Irv gave me his big grin. "You didn't have to say it, little man." He tapped his temple. "I figured it out all by myself."

"Yeah," I said, letting Big Irv make his bed so he could lie in it later. "I guess you did."

"So tell me more."

"About what?" I asked. "Our other amenities? There's salon-quality shampoo in—"

"Smilin' Sam!"

"Oh. Okay. He's a big, hollow Muffler Man statue that, once upon a time, my grandfather painted up to look like Uncle Sam for the Fourth of July."

"And the Sneemer brothers seemed interested in this particular piece?"

"Yes, sir. Maybe they just like mufflers, even

though he's not actually holding one anymore. He just sort of stands there, empty-handed."

"Or maybe," said Big Irv, "the two brothers know that their accomplice, Miss Sheila Bailey, hid the stolen jewels inside your hollow statue."

"No," I said. "They didn't mention anything about jewelry."

"Of course they didn't," said Big Irv with a smile that looked like a smirk. He turned to Mom. "Ma'am? I'll write you a check for five thousand dollars—right here, right now—if you sell that Smilin' Sam statue to me instead of the auction company. The used-car dealer can get one of those AirDancer balloons with the floppy bodies."

"Oh, you really don't want to waste your money," said Mom.

Time for me to hop in. "Wait a second, Mr. Irv. Do *you* think the bad guys hid their stolen jewelry inside our statue?"

Big Irv pulled out a checkbook. "I don't think I should tell you what I think, little man."

"But," I said, "if you find the stolen items, you'll give us our finder's fee because we gave you a good lead, right? One percent of the one-hundred-and-fifty-thousand-dollar reward. That's fifteen hundred dollars."

"Heh, heh, heh. Has somebody been talking with Amalgamated Insurance?"

"Yes, sir."

"Tell you what, little man—I'll give you your finder's fee right now, before anybody actually finds anything, because Big Irv has a big heart." He ripped out the check he'd been writing and started writing another one. "Here you go, Ms. Wilkie. Six thousand, five hundred dollars."

"I really don't think—"

"Stop thinking, ma'am. Try being smart instead."

Oooh.

Mom did not like it when Big Irv (or anybody) said something like that. I could tell by how narrow and crinkly her eyes got all of a sudden.

Then she smiled. Took the check. "Why, thank you, Mr. Irv. Smilin' Sam is all yours."

"Good. I need to make a few calls, organize a truck and a crew of movers. . . ."

"You do that," I said. "Drag Smilin' Sam out of here and cut him open! He's right behind the Putt-Putt golf course. You can't miss him. He's almost as tall as you."

The private investigator rubbed his hands together and hurried out of the office. "Thanks, folks. Pleasure doing business with you."

As he bustled out the lobby door, Gloria strolled in.

"Who's he?" she asked.

"A big jerk," said Mom.

"Better known as Big Irv," I added.

"The private investigator working for the insurance company?" asked Gloria.

"Yep."

"How come you two know so much about all of this?" asked Mom.

I shrugged. "We watch way too much TV."

"What did Big Irv want?" asked Gloria.

"A tip on the jewels," I said.

"Did you guys give him one?"

"I believe," said Mom, straightening her blouse, "Big Irv got exactly what he deserved. Excuse me. I have a bank deposit slip to fill out."

She went into her office and closed the door.

"So," I said to Gloria, "you know that statue Mom thought she'd only be able to sell for a hundred bucks?"

"The one we ruined?"

"Yep," I said proudly. "We just sold it for sixty-five hundred dollars."

"Even though it wasn't at the motel in 1973?"

"Oops," I said. "Big Irv forgot to ask about that. And you know what? We forgot to mention it." Big Irv is going to be hugely disappointed when he cuts open that Muffler Man."

"Caveat emptor," said Gloria. "That's Latin for 'let the buyer beware.' Oldest rule in the business book."

"Is that why it's in Latin?" I asked.

"I guess."

We were laughing when two men in matching green overalls stepped into the lobby.

"Excuse me," said the one with a clipboard. "We're from the Roadside Americana Auction Company."

I nodded. "Let me go get my mom."

I knocked on her office door.

"What is it?" Mom asked, coming out to join us.

I hooked a thumb at the gentlemen in the green jumpsuits.

"We're from Roadside Americana," said Mr. Clipboard.

"Oh, right," said Mom. "Today's the day."

"You folks have a nice collection. Some rare finds."

"Thank you," said Mom. "My dad put it together."

I could hear the lump in her throat. It sounded like it was the same size as mine.

Because to save the Wonderland, we had to sell off all the stuff that made it so wonderful.

Say Good-bye to Wonderland

An hour later, Gloria and I stood in the parking lot, watching Big Irv and some other big guys load Smilin' Sam into the back of a moving van.

Meanwhile, the two men in green jumpsuits barked orders to a whole team of other guys in green jumpsuits, who were loading everything else onto *their* trucks. The Roadside Americana Auction Company had sent a fleet of six cargo haulers plus a crane to hoist everything up onto their flatbeds.

The jackalope was the first to go. The rocket ship was next. Our parking lot was starting to look like the saddest circus train ever.

Behind us, we heard the squeak of metal. Big Irv's movers were closing up the panel doors on the back of their vehicle.

"You think Big Irv will see that 1976 plaque on the base anytime soon?" asked Gloria.

"Nah. Probably not until they unload Smilin' Sam wherever they're taking him."

"Poor guy," said Gloria. "He's in for a bad case of buyer's remorse."

"Buyer's what?"

"Remorse. It's another business buzzword. Means he'll realize he paid way too much for Smilin' Sam. Might start bawling his eyes out."

"Not necessarily," I said. "Maybe he wants to quit being a P.I. and open up a muffler shop."

Yep. Gloria and I were cracking jokes because it was just so sad watching the Wonderland being dismantled.

Grandpa wandered over to join us.

"Sad day, huh, kiddos?" he said.

I nodded. "The saddest. But at least we get to keep the motel."

Grandpa sighed. "Maybe. Maybe not. Even after selling all the statues and the Hawaiian Happy-Stinky

Fruit—plus renting out the ride-on train—we're still coming up short."

"What's the deficit?" asked Gloria.

"Forty thousand dollars."

"What?" I said. "Then why are we even selling all this stuff?"

"Because," said Gloria, "it's better to be forty K in the hole instead of one hundred. Correct?"

Grandpa nodded.

"We're so sorry, Grandpa," I said.

"Nothing to be sorry about. You two tried your best. We all did. I guess I never should've taken out that loan."

"We never should've chased after that stupid jewelry," I said. "We should've concentrated on the dinosaur egg hunt instead of playing a long shot like that."

Grandpa put his hand on my shoulder. "Don't beat yourself up, kiddo. You and Gloria did more to save the Wonderland than anybody else. Who knows? We still have three weeks. Maybe my lottery numbers will finally pay off. Maybe the bank will look the other way, give us some more time. . . ."

"Maybe," I said, faking a smile.

But I knew better.

Gloria and I had heard the banker and the real estate developer scheming. They didn't want us to pay back the loan. They wanted to take over our oceanfront property and bulldoze our motel.

● ● ●

A couple of hours later, five big rigs loaded up with strapped-down statuary rumbled out of the parking lot.

There was one truck still to be packed. Another guy in green work clothes came over to us.

"Excuse me, sir," he said to Grandpa. "We're gonna start cleaning out your workshop. Pack up the train. It'll be our last load."

Grandpa nodded. "The door's unlocked. Have at it." He turned to us. "Who wants one last free ice-cream cone? They're not picking up the swirl-cone dispenser until tomorrow."

Gloria and I both raised our hands.

"Follow me," said Grandpa.

We walked to the pool.

"How about we all do one last Croaky Karaoke, too?" I cracked.

"An excellent suggestion," said Grandpa.

Except Freddy the Frog wasn't poolside anymore.

And all we saw was the empty spot where the big green waterslide used to squat.

Catch the Last Train

While the Roadside Americana crew finished clearing out Grandpa's workshop, I went up to room 233 to hang with Gloria and her dad.

"Tough break, team," said Mr. Ortega in his sportscaster voice as he looked out the window. "Personally, I miss seeing that big mouse nibbling his giant cheese wedge back there. It's how I remembered where I parked: right next to the large rodent. Did they take Stinky Beard, too?"

I nodded. "Stinky Beard. The rocket ship. Dino the Dinosaur. Even our Happy the Clown gumball machine. They took everything."

"And," said Gloria, "even though P.T. swung a sweet deal for Smilin' Sam, his mom still doesn't have enough to pay off the bank. They're forty thousand short."

Mr. Ortega shook his head. "The thrill of victory. The agony of defeat. You win some, you lose some. . . ."

"Do you think you guys at WTSP could host a telethon or something for us?" I asked Mr. Ortega.

He cocked his head sideways like he was thinking about it. "Hmmm. No."

"This stinks worse than Stinky Beard's bean-burrito butt," said Gloria, flopping down on a bed.

"We should've done more." I flopped down on the sofa.

"Well," said Mr. Ortega, "as they often say in the losers' locker room, it just wasn't meant to be. You kids came up a little short, but you have nothing to be ashamed of. The ball just didn't bounce your way. Sure, it's a bitter pill to swallow and the plane ride home will be awfully long. . . ."

"Dad?" said Gloria. "This is our home. We're not getting on a plane anytime soon."

"My bad. Just practicing my losing-locker-room catchphrases for when I make it to ESPN." Mr. Ortega pulled back the curtains and looked out the window again. "Huh. I didn't know you guys had a train."

"Yep," I said. "The Wonder World Express. Grand-pa's renting it to some tourist attraction."

"Guess they want to try it before they buy it," said Gloria, who had a few clichés of her own.

"They're pushing it up a ramp," said Mr. Ortega. "Strapping it down. Now the crew is climbing into the cab of their truck. Closing their doors. *Ka-THUNK!*"

I had to smile. Mr. Ortega just couldn't resist giving us the play-by-play.

"*VROOM!* The engine has fired up. There's the exhaust fumes. The lurch. And off they go."

He let go of the drapes and stepped away from the window.

"So where was Happy Town?" he asked.

"Huh?"

"The caboose on the train. There was a sign on the back: 'Follow Me to Happy Town!' Was that like a happy little village filled with gnomes and dwarves or something?"

"I don't know. You'd have to ask Grandpa."

Mr. Ortega grabbed his Windbreaker. "Can't right now. Filling in for Chuck on the eleven o'clock newscast. See you later, hon."

"Have a good show, Dad."

He breezed out of the room.

And that's when it hit me. "Happy Town!"

I raced to the window. Threw open the curtains.

The Wonder World Express chugged across the parking lot on the back of a flatbed truck.

I saw the caboose!

"P.T.?" said Gloria. "What's up?"

"The jewels! They're on that train."

"Wha-hut?"

"Remember what Sheila wrote on the back of Sidney Sneemer's postcard?"

"Sure. She called him a hunk muffin."

"Before that. 'With your blowhard brother out of the picture, the two of us can book a one-way ticket to Happy Town.' Then she added, 'Follow my tracks'!"

"The train!" gasped Gloria. "Train tracks! Happy Town!"

"Exactly! Come on. We need to stop that truck!"

We raced out of the room, tore along the balcony, and bounded down two flights of metal steps. We reached the landing at the bottom, rounded a corner, and—right there in the breezeway near the ice machine—froze.

Because the Sneemer brothers were back.

"Just the two punks we was lookin' for," sneered Stanley. "Where the heck is Smilin' Sam?"

Hooray for Dollywood

Gloria and I both took a step backward. We bumped into the humming ice machine.

"Where's the statue of the big doofus with the beard and the work boots?" asked Stanley.

"That plastic galoot was our favorite," added Sidney.

My mental wheels were spinning again. I could tell the Sneemers to go find Big Irv. But the Sneemers were violent criminals. If they found Big Irv and Smilin' Sam, they might do something criminally violent.

"Funny you should ask," I said. "You see, we had a giant liquidation sale."

"What?"

"Everything had to go. It was a major, one-day-only event."

Yes, I was channeling a carpet commercial I'd seen on TV.

"You sold the statues?" asked Stanley.

"Is that why the mouse is missing from the parking lot?" asked Sid.

"Yes, sir. No reasonable offer was refused. Our blowout prices were so low we couldn't even advertise them."

Stanley took a step forward. Behind us, an avalanche of cubes tumbled into the ice machine. That'll startle you.

"We don't like hearing this," said Stanley.

"Especially after spending the night on a jail cot," added Sidney.

"That map you gave us weren't no good, kid."

Gloria was starting to tremble a little.

I played it cool. "Sorry. Maybe your baby sister, Sheila, wanted to send you two on a wild-goose chase as a goof. I don't have a sister, but my friend Pinky Nelligan does. He says sisters do mean stuff like that all the time just to drive their brothers nuts."

Sidney grabbed me by the front of my shirt. "Where is it, kid?"

"Where's what?"

"The statue!"

"Dollywood!" I blurted.

"Where?"

"Dollywood. It's an amusement park in Tennessee.

Near a town called Pigeon Forge. They have all sorts of rides and attractions. They needed a Muffler Man, so we sold them Smilin' Sam. I think they're going to paint him up and turn him into a mountain man who plays in a jug band."

Yes, once upon a time, my mom and I actually went on a vacation up I-75 to Dollywood. So I had some details to flesh out my tall tale.

"When did they take off?" asked Stanley.

"Maybe an hour ago."

"Half an hour," said Gloria. "Forty-five minutes, tops."

I nodded. "Maybe you can catch up with them at a weigh station or a rest stop."

"Then, if you really want the statue," said Gloria, "maybe you can offer to buy it for more money than they paid."

Sidney smiled. "Yeah. Right. That's what we're gonna do. Offer to *buy* it."

He cracked his knuckles. Then he cracked the joints in his neck.

"So, Stanley? You know what I'm thinking?"

"Yeah, Sid. Road trip."

"See you later, kids."

"Pack your bags, Sid. I'll settle up with the front desk. We're checking out of this two-bit fleabag."

"Have a pleasant journey, Mr. Joneses," I said with a smile. "And give my regards to Dollywood."

"Yeah, right. We'll do that, too."

The two brothers shambled away.

Gloria and I stayed where we were until bags were dragged out of rooms, bills were paid, trunk lids were slammed shut, and two car engines cranked to life.

"Guess they're taking separate vehicles," I said.

"Can you blame them?" asked Gloria. "I wouldn't want to ride with either one of those guys."

"Come on," I said. "We need to talk to Mom. She might know who's renting the train. And let's just hope it isn't Dollywood!"

Lions, Tigers, and Cheetahs (Oh, My)

It was nearly seven-thirty and the sun was starting to set.

Gloria and I hurried into the motel office.

Mom was behind the counter, running numbers through her calculator again. She stared at the curled paper spewing out of it and gave us her report: somehow, we were now *forty-one* thousand dollars short instead of forty.

"What happened?" I asked.

"Families that checked in because of Freddy the Frog are checking out because they saw Freddy being shipped off to who knows where on the back of a truck."

"You don't know where the statues are going?" asked Gloria.

"Not really," said Mom. "Well, not all of them, anyway. The auction company will probably take them to their warehouse and try to match them with bidders all over the country."

"What about the Wonder World Express?" I asked. "Any idea where Grandpa's old train is headed?"

"Yes. That one, I do know."

"Excellent!"

Mom gave me another one of her looks.

"Oh-kay. If you say so. We're renting it to a small zoo over in Tampa. The zoo wanted to give the train a trial run before they committed to buying it. Actually, it's a sanctuary, not a zoo, so the animals come first. They don't let people wander around unescorted."

"That's good," said Gloria. "I guess."

"Oh, it's definitely good. It's a safe haven for exotic large cats. You know—lions, cheetahs, tigers, leopards. Anyway, they thought it might be fun to put in a train. Especially for the kids so they could ride around and see all the wild animals without getting too close." Mom went to the brochure rack. "Here you go. You can read all about them. Might be fun to visit once we figure out where we're moving."

"We're moving?" I said.

"Well, P.T., when the bank takes over the motel,

I don't think they're going to let us keep living here rent-free. They might even want to tear the building down."

Fact: from what Gloria and I had heard in the parking lot, we knew that was exactly what they wanted to do.

Double fact: somehow, we were going to stop them!

"Thanks for this," I said, tapping the Wild Cat Safariland brochure. "Come on, Gloria. We need to go see Grandpa."

"Do you guys want dinner?" asked Mom.

"No thanks," I said. "I'm not really hungry. We had a big lunch."

"Um, what are you serving?" asked Gloria.

"Do you like fish tacos?" said Mom.

"Love 'em. So does my dad."

"Great. I'll grill up some grouper."

I grabbed Gloria by the elbow and said to Mom, "We'll call Mr. Ortega at the TV station and tell him to drop by after work. You two can have a late-night, grown-up-style fish taco dinner together. It might be kind of late. . . ."

Mom smiled. "That would be kind of nice. You sure you kids will be okay?"

"We'll be fine. We have video games that need to be played. Start marinating the grouper."

I practically pulled Gloria out the door.

The second we were outside, she said, "For the record, P.T., I *love* fish tacos."

"We can eat later." I waved the brochure. "Right now, we need Grandpa to drive us to Tampa!"

Tampa Time

We went into the workshop and told Grandpa that we thought the stolen jewelry from the Miami hotel heist of 1973 was hidden on the Wonder World Express train.

"That's why Sheila Bailey rode around the property with you every day," I said. "She was scouting out hiding places for the loot."

Grandpa took a long, slow sip of his Cel-Ray soda.

Then he took another.

Then he belched.

"She didn't ride the train so she could spend quality time with me?"

"I'm sure that was one of her reasons," said Gloria.

"Will the concession stand be open at this Wild Cat Safariland?" asked Grandpa.

"Um," I said, "I think the whole park will be closed. We'll probably have to sneak in."

"Fine. I'll pack some bologna-and-mustard sandwiches."

"We really don't have time, Grandpa."

"There's always time for bologna and mustard, P.T. Besides, if my stomach's growling too close to all those big cats, they may take it personally. Now, if you two give me a hand with the provisions . . ."

Grandpa, Gloria, and I grabbed the ingredients out of his tiny workshop refrigerator.

"I'm sorry about your angel in the polka-dot scarf, Grandpa," I said.

"She was no angel, P.T. She was just giving me the old razzle-dazzle."

We slapped stinky pink disks of pressed meat on spongy bread, fart-squirted it with swirls of yellow mustard, and topped the mess off with another slab of soft white bread. We wrapped six sandwiches in wax paper (two for each of us was Grandpa's dinner plan), packed them in a brown paper sack, and grabbed a cold six-pack of Dr. Brown's Cel-Ray soda from the fridge, too.

We dashed out to Grandpa's wood-paneled surfer-mobile. Well, Gloria and I dashed. Grandpa more or less ambled. He also burped some more.

"We should probably tell your mother where we're going," said Grandpa when he climbed behind the wheel.

I shook my head. "Bad idea."

"How so?"

"Mom's the grown-up in the family, remember?"

"Right. And it would be totally irresponsible of me to drive you kids to a wild-animal park after dark."

"Correct."

"P.T.? You picked the right man for the job."

He cranked the ignition.

We were off on another adventure.

● ● ●

We cruised across the Pinellas Bayway, took the ramp for I-275 north, and headed across the three-mile-long Gandy Bridge spanning the bay between St. Petersburg and Tampa. Since we had at least twenty more minutes of driving to do, I told Grandpa everything.

About the Miami Palm Tree Hotel heist. About Stanley and Sidney Sneemer. About Sheila holding the hot loot.

I told Grandpa how she had double-crossed Stanley because she'd had a crush on Sidney. How Stanley had snitched out both of them. How Sheila had hidden the jewels in the train, then died behind bars in the state pen before anybody discovered where she'd stashed the loot. How Stanley and Sidney had just gotten out of jail. How they had Wonder World postcards with clues scribbled across the back. How the clues had led us to the Wonder World Express train.

When I was finished, he said, "Good detective work, kiddos. Does anybody else know about this?"

"Not yet," I said. "We sent Big Irv, the detective who's been working the case for the insurance company, off on a wild-goose chase with Smilin' Sam."

"And P.T. sent the Sneemer brothers to Dollywood," added Gloria.

I shrugged. "They might enjoy the Barnstormer roller coaster. I know I did."

"So we have the jewels all to ourselves?" asked Grandpa.

"Yep," I said. "And we can cash them in for a one-hundred-and-fifty-thousand-dollar reward!"

"I like the sound of that," said Grandpa. "We can use it to pay off the bank loan!"

"Exactly," I said. "But first we have to find where Sheila hid the jewels on the train."

"We also have to avoid being eaten alive by lions," added Gloria.

"Right. That, too."

Cat-astrophe?

We parked near the entrance to Wild Cat Safariland.

There was only one other car in the gravel parking lot. It was near a gate that I figured was the employee entrance to the animal sanctuary. That meant at least one person (maybe a security guard or a lion tamer) was still on the property.

All the signs out front were dark. The place had closed hours earlier.

"That car probably belongs to somebody we don't want to bump into," I whispered as we quietly made our way toward the gloomy entrance. The only light came from the flickering fluorescent tube inside an ancient vending machine. "There's probably a security guard on patrol."

"There's your security guard," Gloria whispered back. "In his cage!"

The caged lion gave us a warning growl.

"How many large cats live here?" asked Grandpa, who was toting our sandwich bag.

"Several hundred." Yes, I'd read the whole brochure.

Since the train had just been shipped to Safariland, we wouldn't find it waiting for us at Catmandu Junction, or whatever they'd eventually call their loading depot. There weren't any train tracks ringing the property yet, either. We were basically looking for a needle in a haystack where all the hay smelled like a litter box somebody should've scooped out weeks before.

We slipped under the chain draped across the entry and moved into the animal sanctuary, treading very carefully along the asphalt trails winding through the cat enclosures.

Fortunately, the moon was bright, so we could see where we were going and who was staring at us with glassy eyes: all sorts of rumbling, grumbling lions and tigers and cheetahs and jaguars and panthers (which, by the way, would be very hard to see in the dark if their eyeballs didn't glow like bicycle reflectors). Some of the cats were pacing in their pens. Others swatted at us with paws the size of catchers' mitts. A couple roared. Several stretched open their jaws so we could check out their glistening dental work. Their teeth were shinier than Mr. Ortega's.

"Anybody else hungry?" said Grandpa when we reached a cluster of picnic tables.

"Are you serious?" I asked.

"No, I'm starving. I haven't had my dinner yet."

He sat down. Popped open another Cel-Ray soda. Unwrapped a sandwich. Gloria and I just stood there, rolling our eyes in disbelief.

"I'm sorry," said Grandpa. "I have to watch my blood sugar. If I don't eat—"

A nearby lion roared.

We whipped around. The big beast was frantically sniffing the air. What can I say? Bologna is one of the stinkiest deli meats ever invented. It's right up there with liverwurst.

"Sorry, kitty," said Grandpa, smacking his lips. "This is *my* supper."

I heard the squeak of rusty metal behind us.

"What does y'all think you're doin' back here?"

A bright beacon spotlighted Grandpa as he licked yellow mustard off his fingers.

A scrawny man in a filthy safari suit and a Tampa Bay Rays baseball cap trained his flashlight on us. He stood in front of a tiger cage with a gate that didn't look completely locked or even closed. The man took a step forward and spit out a gob of something brown.

"I asked you what you was doin', old-timer."

"Eating my supper," said Grandpa.

"Oh. Did ya bring a sam'wich for me?"

Safari Bob

"I was just tucking me in an ornery tiger," said the skinny man in the safari costume, tugging on the bill of his baseball cap. "That'll work up your appetite somethin' fierce."

He looked to be maybe forty-some years old. He also looked like he didn't shave on a regular basis. Judging from the scroll of stitching over his chest pocket, his name was Bob.

I like havin' me a name tag. Helps me remember who I am.

"Um, Bob, I think you forgot to shut that ornery tiger's cage there," I said, gesturing toward the chain-link fence behind him.

"You tryin' to tell me how to do my job, son?"

"No, sir. I just . . ."

Bob worked his nose through the air like the lion had done when it first smelled Grandpa's bologna.

"That bologna you're eatin' there, pops?"

"Yes, sir," said Grandpa, wadding up his wax paper. "We have Dr. Brown's Cel-Ray soda, too."

Bob squinted. "Dr. Who's what?"

"Dr. Brown's Cel-Ray soda."

"What's it taste like?"

"Celery," said Grandpa.

"Shoot. Who'd want to drink a sodie that tastes like a salad?"

"Grandpa," I said. "And cats. Well, my cat. Cheeseball. The smell of celery drives her nuts." I reached into the supermarket sack to pull out another wrapped sandwich. "Here you go, Bob. We brought several."

"Thank you kindly." He took the sandwich. "But we're closed. Y'all can't be having a picnic out here till tomorrow."

"Well, Bob," I said, "we're really here for the train."

"What train?"

"The one you guys rented from Grandpa," I said.

"You're a used-train dealer, pops?"

Grandpa laughed. "Not usually. Just for today."

"You see," I said, acting even politer than I had on TV, "my grandfather, Walt Wilkie—"

"No way!" said Bob. "You're *the* Walt Wilkie? From Walt Wilkie's Wonder World?"

Grandpa stood up and straightened his clothes a little. "Yes. Have we met?"

"Yes, sir," said Bob. "But I cain't blame you for not rememberin'. I was knee-high to a grasshopper at the time. Only eight or nine years old. Me and my family came to Wonder World for your bicentennial celebration. Had our picture taken with that big ol' smilin' Uncle Sam feller. Sir, you even let me twirl a sparkler. Best vacation we ever had."

"Why, thank you," said Grandpa. "It was my pleasure to create memories for you and your family." He took a slight bow.

"Remember the train?" I asked.

"Sure do. Chugged around the park all the way to Happy Town, where there was all these mechanical clown dolls. I remember they moved and waved and juggled and such. It was kind of creepy."

"We changed the clowns to glow-in-the-dark unicorns in 1977," said Grandpa.

Bob nodded. "Smart move. Unicorns ain't half as creepy as clowns."

"Well, now you guys have the Wonder World train right here at Wild Cat Safariland," I said. "We shipped it over this afternoon."

"Is that so? I reckon if it just come in, they probably put it in storage. Back yonder in that there Quonset hut we got."

"Can you take us to the train?" I asked. "I lost something on it."

Bob took off his baseball cap and scratched his head. "Huh?"

His Tampa Bay Rays hat gave me an idea for my next story.

"You see, sir, for years, that old ride-on train was just collecting dust and cobwebs in Grandpa's workshop. I sort of used it as a hiding place for my prized possessions. But I made a small mistake: I forgot to tell Grandpa."

"So," said Gloria, catching on to where I was going with this, "if you don't mind, Bob, we'd like to search the train to see if P.T. can find his prized possession. Since Safariland is only renting the train, it is technically still property of the Wonderland Motel and—"

"Uh-huh," said Bob, spitting out another wet gob the color of melted chocolate. "What exactly did you lose, Petey?"

Fortunately, I've been a Rays fan since forever. I had the details I needed to sell another bit.

"My mint-condition 2006 Bowman Draft Picks Chrome Evan Longoria card!"

Bob nearly lost his jaw. "No way. Longoria weren't even called up to Tampa Bay till 2008. You have his draft pick card? Dang. That's worth more than his rookie card."

"I know!" I gushed. "That's why I need to find it."

"If you do," said Bob, "can I hold it? Maybe take a selfie?"

"You bet."

"Then come on, son. Follow me. We have a train to catch!"

Mmm. Bologna and celery. I love me some bologna and celery.

Lost and Found

Bob took us to a building that looked like a half-buried semicircle made out of corrugated steel. It had two wide-open entrances: one at the front, one at the back.

Bob flicked a switch, lights thumped on, and there it was: the Wonder World Express!

"Woo-hoo!" said Gloria. "We found it."

"Where's your baseball card, Petey?" asked Bob.

"Actually," said Gloria, "his name is P.T."

"Huh?"

"Never mind."

"So," said Grandpa, studying the engine, passenger cars, and caboose that made up the train, "where do you think she hid them?"

"Who hid what?" said Bob, who thought we were looking for a single baseball card.

"My sister," I said, even though I don't have one. "She, uh, always sneaks into Grandpa's workshop and finds the stuff I hide so she can re-hide it somewhere else."

Bob shook his head. "Sisters. Am I right?"

"You sure are," said Gloria.

"So now," I said, "we need to search the whole train! Because even though I know I hid my baseball card in the smokestack—"

"Dang, son. You hid a mint-condition 2006 Evan Longoria card inside a smokestack?" Bob sounded horrified.

"It's laminated," I assured him. "And sealed inside a ziplock bag."

Bob nodded. "All righty, then."

"We might be a while," I told him. "Maybe you should go enjoy your sandwich."

"Reckon I might do that. But don't forget, Petey: I want that selfie. Me and Evan Longoria."

"You've got it, sir!"

"Want a soda?" asked Grandpa, offering him a can of Cel-Ray.

"No thanks. I only eat celery when it's acting like a canoe for my pimento cheese."

Bob strolled out of the Quonset hut to enjoy his bologna on white bread at one of the picnic tables.

When he was gone, the three of us split up and started our search. Since Grandpa knew more about the train's engine than anybody else did, he checked every nook and cranny of the locomotive. Gloria and I worked together in the passenger cars. We pulled up seat cushions. Checked out all the corners. We even crawled under the carriages to see if something was hidden underneath or strapped to the wheels.

We were at it for fifteen, maybe twenty, minutes.

We found nothing—except some antique kernels of shriveled popcorn and some clever squirrel's stash of nuts.

"The jewels have to be in the caboose," I said.

"Or," said Gloria, "Miss Sheila 'Boom-Boom' Bailey is laughing at us all right now. You, me, your grandfather, Sidney, Stanley—even Big Irv."

We pried up the cushions on the two bench seats facing each other in the caboose. Their lids were on hinges.

"Excellent hiding places," said Gloria. She reached inside her seat and found Grandpa's rumpled and sweat-stained engineer's cap.

"Eureka!" said Grandpa, wiping the grease off his hands with a rag he'd found. "I've been looking for that."

"What've you got on your side, P.T.?" asked Gloria.

I shined my iPhone flashlight around inside the empty cabinet under the backseat of the caboose.

"Nothing," I said. "It's like an empty toy chest.

It would've been so easy for Sheila to flip up this seat and . . ."

My light hit something.

A crumpled paper bag.

"Hang on. There's a bag back here."

"Grab it!" said Gloria.

I did. I was so excited my fingers wouldn't work. I was fumbling with the flaps, trying to work it open.

"What's inside?" Grandpa asked eagerly.

Finally, I rolled the bag open. Stuck my hand inside. And wished I hadn't.

"Gross," I mumbled.

It was one of Grandpa's bologna-and-yellow-mustard-on-white-bread sandwiches. The bread had black mold splotches on it. And the pink meat had shriveled up and turned kind of green. The mustard had long since evaporated. The thing had to be two, maybe three, years old.

"I've been looking for that, too," said Grandpa.

I dropped the bag into the rectangular box and let the cushioned lid slam so I could sit down in the caboose and pout.

"The jewels aren't here," I said. "Maybe they never were."

While I was moping, I finally saw the light.

Actually, I saw the lanterns. Four of them. One on every corner of the caboose. The glass globes were frosted stoplight red.

"Are there lightbulbs inside those lanterns?" I asked.

"No," said Grandpa. "I never went in for the whole blinking-light business. This is a train, not a Christmas tree."

In other words, the globes were empty.

I climbed out and started unscrewing the glass shades from their metal bases.

Three of the lanterns were empty.

But the last one I unscrewed?

There was a rusty-hinged Band-Aid box inside it.

What'd you find in that one?

Cobwebs and spider eggs.

Are the eggs jewel-encrusted?

Greetings from Miami

When I popped the metal lid on the Band-Aid box, I saw a folded-over envelope stuffed with something.

"Is it the jewels?" asked Gloria.

"I'm not sure." I worked the envelope out of the tight tin container. "It's motel stationery, like we used to have in all the desks at the Wonderland," I said, examining the envelope. "It's from the Miami Palm Tree Hotel!"

"That's where they stole the jewelry!" exclaimed Gloria.

"Open it, P.T.," urged Grandpa. "Open it! Hurry!"

I slid the Band-Aid box into my back pocket and tried to rip open the envelope.

"She sealed it up with packing tape," I said as I struggled to tear the thing open.

"Give it to me," said Gloria.

I handed her the envelope. She ripped it open. With her teeth.

Gloria gasped.

"Is it?" I asked.

Gloria nodded.

"Really?" said Grandpa.

And Gloria just smiled. "Hold out your hand, P.T." I did.

And sparkling jewelry tumbled out of the torn envelope like peanut M&M'S pouring out of the bag.

"We need to get out of here," I said. "Now!"

"Bob is going to be so disappointed that you didn't show him your baseball card," said Gloria.

"With this much loot," I said, jiggling the clinking jewelry in my hand, "I'll buy him two of his own."

"Careful, P.T.," said Grandpa. "Put that stuff somewhere safe."

"Good point." I did as Grandpa suggested while he and Gloria screwed the lamp covers back onto their brackets. I folded over the envelope from the Miami Palm Tree Hotel and tossed it into the brown paper sack with the remaining sandwiches and Cel-Ray soda cans.

We were all set to leave.

And, of course, that's when Bob came back.

With Big Irv.

"Eh, heh, heh, heh. Hello, little man."

I wiggle-waggled my fingers at him. "Hey there." I turned to Bob. "Well, we couldn't find my baseball card. Guess my sister swiped it. Thanks for letting us look. Buh-bye."

I stepped forward.

Big Irv blocked my path.

"What's in the grocery sack, little man?"

"Bologna sandwiches. And this weird celery soda Grandpa and maybe two other people in the whole world actually like."

"It's not weird," said Grandpa defensively. "It's wonderful. The two are sometimes related."

"You find them jewels?" asked Bob. "Big Irv told me all about what you folks was really in here searchin' for. Diamonds and emeralds and rings filled with rubies and such like that."

Big Irv reached into his suit coat and pulled out the fattest roll of cash I've ever seen.

"Here you go, Bob. Your finder's fee. Five thousand dollars." He peeled off five thousand-dollar bills.

Seriously.

Grover Cleveland's face was on them.

My cranky history teacher, Mr. Frumpkes, might've been surprised that I recognized the guy who was the twenty-second and twenty-fourth president of the United States, but I did. Maybe he'll give me extra-credit points.

"Dang," said Bob, staring at the stack of cash. "Didn't know I was gonna hit the lottery tonight."

"Why don't you head on home, Bob?" suggested Big Irv.

"Cain't. Shift ain't over till tomorrow morning."

"Fine. Quit."

"Cain't."

"Yes, you can."

Big Irv peeled off ten more Grover Clevelands.

"Dang. That's my kind of retirement fund!

See y'all folks later. Don't let a big ol' cat bite you in the butt."

Bob scampered out of the Quonset hut.

When Big Irv was certain Bob was gone, he tapped another bulge in his suit coat.

This one didn't look like a roll of cash.

This one looked more like a gun.

Let's Make Another Deal

"Heh, heh, heh," Big Irv chuckled. "Did you seriously think you could outsmart me, little man?"

He pulled back his suit coat to show us the pistol tucked into a shoulder holster.

Gloria and Grandpa took a step backward. For whatever reason, I didn't. Maybe because we were so close to saving the Wonderland, I couldn't let anything stand in my way, not even a giant named Big Irv.

"Quick question, Mr. Irv," I said. "My new friend Gloria here has been teaching me a little about business. You just gave Bob fifteen thousand dollars. That's *ten* percent of the one-hundred-and-fifty-thousand-dollar reward being offered by the insurance company. Your original finder's fee was *one* percent. What's up with the big change?"

Big Irv grinned. "Who said I'm giving those

jewels to the insurance company, little man? Do you know how much five million dollars' worth of diamonds, emeralds, and rubies from 1973 would be worth today?"

"Twenty-seven million." Gloria and I said it together.

Big Irv pulled out his roll of thousand-dollar bills again. "Now, I already gave you folks sixty-five hundred dollars for a worthless plastic statue. Wasn't anything inside it but mouse droppings and seagull poop."

Grandpa nodded. "The seagulls liked to sit on Smilin' Sam's head. There's a hole up top where we used to anchor his hat. Just like on Mr. Potato Head."

"Whatever," said Big Irv. "I'll give you nine thousand more, putting you at fifteen thousand five hundred. Five hundred more than I just gave Bob. All you have to do is give me what you've got in that grocery bag, little man."

"Can I ask another question first?" I said.

"Make it fast. I don't have all night."

"How'd you find us?"

"Easy. While the movers loaded that good-for-nothing hunk of fiberglass junk into the truck, I attached GPS trackers to the bumpers of your mother's and grandfather's vehicles."

"You're a pro, sir," I said. "A true professional. I respect that. You do your job and you do it well."

"Little man?"

"Yes, sir?"

"You talk too much. Just take your cash. Give me the jewels."

"I'm not sure nine thousand extra is enough," I said. "We should split the jewels fifty-fifty. After all, we're the ones who actually figured out the clues and found the Sneemer brothers' stash."

Big Irv wasn't grinning or chuckling anymore. In fact, he was starting to look ticked off.

So I kept going. I can be extremely annoying when I try.

Remember how I said some stories have more power than all the facts you can find on Google? I was about to put that theory to the test, big-time.

"By the way," I said, "'Big Irv' is a very interesting name. Is that what was written on your birth certificate? Were you a large infant, Irving?"

"Give me the bag, little man."

"My grandfather gave me my name. Phineas Taylor. I'm named after P. T. Barnum. You would've liked Barnum, Big Irv. He owned an elephant named Jumbo. I guess my dad might've given me a different name, but he was out of town at the time, over in Bangladesh, training Bengal tigers with bologna bits, because it's surprising how much tigers love bologna. Bologna reminds me of catnip, except it's a cold cut."

Big Irv looked like he was ready to explode.

"That's why my grandfather eats so many bolo-gna sandwiches—in memory of my dad and his work with the royal Bengal tigers over in—"

Big Irv whipped out his pistol. Aimed it at the ceiling. And fired.

"Shut! Up!"

The gunshot boomed like thunder under the Quonset hut's curved steel ceiling. It was as if some-one had just banged a gong in all our heads.

I heard the big cats outside roar and growl. They reminded me of Cheeseball that time I accidentally dropped her metal food bowl on the floor, where it rattled around and made a racket. Cats don't like loud noises.

"All right already," I shouted so I could hear myself over the ringing in my ears. "Keep your money. We won't tell anybody you found the Sneemer brothers' loot."

"Give me the bag."

"One second. I'm kind of thirsty." I pulled out a can of Dr. Brown's Cel-Ray soda and shook it. "You need to shake it to mix up the celery juice."

"Give. Me. The. Bag!"

I tossed it to him.

He looked inside. Saw the folded-over Miami Palm Tree Hotel envelope. He was about to pull it out of the bag for a quick inspection when a huge tiger roared—maybe ten feet behind him.

Big Irv was so startled he spun around and dropped his pistol.

It was the big cat from that unlocked cage.

The gunshot had woken the tiger up.

It was growling at Big Irv and sniffing the bologna-scented air.

What do you know? So far, my plan was actually working!

I just hoped it didn't get us eaten by a tiger.

Bologna Bait

Big Irv made a move to pick up his pistol.

The tiger roared again. Swatted the air with its humongous paw. Then, hips swaying, it stalked forward.

"Fine," Big Irv said to the big cat. "You can have the pistol. I have another one in my car."

Carefully—very, very carefully—Big Irv backed away from the snarling tiger and eased toward the wide-open rear entrance.

The tiger turned toward me, Gloria, and Grandpa because we were closer and Grandpa definitely reeked of bologna.

I shook my Dr. Brown's soda can one more time.

I popped the top.

The hiss of the spritz made the cat back off, just like a spray bottle does with Cheeseball.

Then I aimed the celery juice geyser toward Big Irv, who was nearly out the back door. The tiger turned to follow the aroma. It started sniffing the air and licking its chops. I was pretty certain the big cat had just picked up the scent of all the juicy bologna tucked inside Big Irv's bag.

Big Irv made his move. He jammed the paper sack under his arm like a football and dashed out of the Quonset hut.

The tiger roared one more time and took off in hot pursuit.

"Good work, P.T.," said Grandpa. "Big Irv won't stop running until he's in Miami."

"Um, P.T.?" said Gloria, raising her hand like we were in school. "As your business advisor, I have to ask: why didn't you take Big Irv's offer of nine thousand dollars in cash?"

"Because I wanted my stupid story to make him so mad he'd fire his weapon. I just hoped he wouldn't fire it at us."

"It worked," said Grandpa.

"I just gave him the old razzle-dazzle!"

Gloria shook her head. "You like living on the edge, don't you?"

"Hey, you're the one who taught me: no risk, no reward."

"That's for the stock market, P.T. Not guns!"

"It would've been dishonest money," said Grandpa. "Ill-gotten gains."

"True," said Gloria. "But the bank wouldn't care. You could've used that money to help pay off the balloon loan, which, hello, is why we've been doing all this crazy stuff in the first place!"

"Come on, you guys," I said. "We need to head out to the parking lot. Make sure Big Irv hasn't been completely mauled."

"*Wha-hut?*"

"The man is carrying a sack of smelly meat while being pursued by a ferocious carnivore,

Gloria. He might need an ambulance. We should call 911."

"We also need some cops to arrest him!" added Gloria. "He just stole all that stolen jewelry!"

We headed out of the steel storage shed just in time to hear a car door slam, a tiger roar, and spinning tires churn up a backward barrage of gravel. The tiger yelped. I think a chunk of rock must've beaned him on the snout.

Big Irv's car tore out of the Safariland parking lot.

"Well," I said, "he's gone. Baseball Card Bob, too. So we still need to call 911. Someone has to put that tiger back in its cage."

Gloria sighed. "I'll make the call." She pulled out her cell phone.

"Ask them to send somebody from animal control," I suggested. "And see if they know anyone at the Amalgamated Insurance Company."

Gloria shot me a puzzled look. "Why?"

"Because they need to give us our one-hundred-and-fifty-thousand-dollar reward."

I pulled the Band-Aid box out of my jeans. Shook it so Gloria and Grandpa could hear the diamonds and emeralds and rubies rattling around inside it.

They were staring at me.

"I took Grandpa's advice," I said with a shrug. "I put the jewels someplace safe. My back pocket."

It's a Wonderful Life

We turned the jewelry over to the insurance company.

They gave us the one-hundred-and-fifty-thousand-dollar reward.

Big Irv?

He got an empty Miami Palm Tree Hotel envelope. It's over forty years old, so maybe it qualifies as an antique. If so, he can sell it on eBay. For five, maybe ten, bucks.

We gave the cops who responded to our 911 call Big Irv's pistol. I think they're going to talk to him about shooting holes in the roofs of other people's Quonset huts.

The Sneemer brothers? I hope they enjoyed their time at Dollywood.

We paid off the balloon loan at the bank a week

early. Somewhere there's a sleazy real estate developer named Arnold weeping.

And all those statues we were going to sell off? With some of the money left over from the reward, we were able to pay the Roadside Americana Auction Company to ship them all back to St. Pete Beach, where they reinstalled every piece in its proper place. Freddy the Frog is back, doing two shows a day. Well, at least on the weekends, when Gloria and I don't have school. Smilin' Sam needed major patching and a paint job (Big Irv had hacked some huge holes into the poor guy), so we decided to go ahead and turn him into Ponce de León, complete with his plumed conquistador helmet, plywood sword, and funny balloon pants. Grandpa loved my Fountain of Tall idea. Gloria had her brand-new Junior Achievement pals at the middle school (where she's now stuck in Mr. Frumpkes's class with me) design and market the bottled Growth Elixir water.

She and her dad are still living at the Wonderland. Tuesday night is our official Family Fish Taco Night together.

And yes, Mom still acts slightly goofy around Mr. Ortega.

After paying off the debt and reinstalling all the old attractions, we still have about thirty thousand dollars left to play with.

Mom wants us to be prudent and save it for a rainy day. We reminded her that this is Florida and it rains nearly every day.

Grandpa wants to use the surplus cash to lay in new train tracks for the Wonderland Express.

I want us to buy some sort of audio-animatronic character, like that Abe Lincoln they have in the Hall of Presidents over at Disney World. Maybe we could do Grover Cleveland talking about what it's like to be on the one-thousand-dollar bill. Better yet, we could bring Stinky Beard the pirate to animated life. Just think of the promotional possibilities during International Talk Like a Pirate Day!

We have to come up with something pretty spectacular, though, because Gloria and I seriously want to win that "Hottest Family Attraction in the Sunshine State" trophy from *Florida Fun in the Sun* magazine.

Fact: we want to beat Disney World.

Double fact: we want to do it for Grandpa.

So, Dad, if you're reading this (because I sort of wrote it so you would), I hope you'll realize what you've been missing all these years. Like I told my friends at school, living in a motel is always exciting.

And guess what. There's a lot more fun in the sun to come—not to mention marvels to behold and stories to be told.

So drop by anytime.

We're having a wonderful time at the Wonderland.

Take a vacation in a book!
Don't miss the next adventure!

"Nonstop hilarity—
five stars!"
—Lincoln Peirce, Big Nate series

Welcome to WONDERLAND

BEACH PARTY SURF MONKEY

CHRIS GRABENSTEIN

New York Times bestselling author of *Escape from Mr. Lemoncello's Library*

Turn the page for a preview!

Excerpt text copyright © 2017 by Chris Grabenstein. Excerpt illustrations
copyright © 2017 by Brooke Allen. Published by Random House Children's Books,
a division of Penguin Random House LLC, New York.

The Grand Tour?

I knew that Aidan had to meet Grandpa.

When it comes to selling the wonders of the Wonderland, nobody does it better than Walt Wilkie.

If, with Aidan Tyler's help, we could turn our motel into a famous movie location landmark, Mom would forget all about selling out to Mr. Conch and moving to Arizona. Too many people from all over the world would want to visit and stay at the Wonderland once it became a movie star.

So I texted Grandpa:

MEET ME BEHIND DINO!

He, of course, *called* me back.

"P.T.?" he said. "What are these words someone's

typing on my telephone screen here? Why is it all of a sudden making funny squiggly sounds?"

Grandpa's new to smartphones.

"Meet us behind Dino!" I told him.

"Why?"

"We have a very important guest."

"Ohhh. Is it the president?"

"No."

"Then it can wait. I'm eating lunch. Bologna and mustard on white bread with pickle relish. You want one?"

"No thanks. Grandpa? Our guest is a major celebrity and he's looking for a motel to use as the setting for his first movie."

"Ooh. They pay for that."

"I know. And nobody bulldozes down motels once they've been in a movie. Hurry!"

I ended the call and poked my head out of the giant dinosaur's tail.

"Looks like everybody's gone. . . ."

Gloria came out after me. Aidan followed her.

"So what's your name, man?" Aidan asked me.

"P.T."

"Solid. Easy to spell. Yo, I'm Aidan Tyler. The Tyes."

"Yeah," said Gloria. "We got that. I'm Gloria Ortega."

"Nice. You a fan?"

"Yes. Of Barbara Corcoran. She's an entrepreneur on *Shark Tank*. You ever watch that show?"

"Girl, I *own* a shark tank. Got me some piranhas in there, too."

"So who's this handsome young fellow?" asked Grandpa, who'd ambled over from his workshop to join us behind Dino. He was clicking his tongue like crazy. I could tell: he had a wad of white bread mustard-glued to the roof of his mouth. Again.

"Grandpa," I said, "this is Aidan Tyler. He's a mega-major superstar."

"Pleased to meet you, young man. I'm Walt Wilkie. And this, my friend, is your lucky day. Behold the Wonderland, the most wondrous motel under the sun!"

Grandpa spread his arms wide open to take in the glory of our motel. Then he smiled. I think he expected an orchestra to swell or fireworks to fill the sky. Something like that.

"Cool," said Aidan. "Nice meeting you, Pops. But I already have a crib."

"Oh, you have a baby in your room?"

"'Crib' is another word for 'place to stay,'" I explained to Grandpa. "Like I told you, Mr. Tyler is in town scouting locations for a new movie."

"It's an off-the-hook remake of those old beach party movies from the 1960s," said Aidan.

"Oh," said Grandpa. "I remember those. And I

remember all the dance moves, too. The Watusi. The Frug. The Shimmy. And, of course, the Swim."

He pinched his nose with one hand, raised the other hand high over his head, and wiggled down like he was diving underwater.

"That's cool, Pops. But this is, like, a total reboot. *Beach Party Surf Monkey*! Starring me, an Academy Award–winning actress, and a monkey."

"There's a monkey in the movie?" said Grandpa, sounding impressed. "Monkeys are good. Funny. Oh, the shtick a monkey can do . . ."

"Yo, this ain't no ordinary monkey, Pops," said Aidan. "This is YouTube sensation Kevin the Monkey!"

Now *I* was impressed.

"Mr. Tyler," I said, "we'd love to have you and Kevin film here. As you can see, the Wonderland is a one-of-a-kind location filled with—"

Aidan's phone thrummed in his board shorts.

"Yo. Gotta book. That's my ride."

He dug out a crinkled business card and handed it to me.

"Call my people. ASAP, dawg. Tomorrow's the big pitch day. Ciao for now."

He strutted out to Gulf Boulevard, where a stretch limo idled at the curb. We followed him.

"So where are you staying?" asked Grandpa.

"Next door. Conch Reef Resort. It's got that new-carpet smell. Plus, they're giving me frequent-stayer points. They also have a world-class buffet with deep-fried cheesy shark bites. I love me some cheesy shark bites. This is the Tyes. I'm out!"

He did a flashy back-and-forth arm thing with the "out."

A burly security guard in a dark suit and sun-glasses opened the back door of the limo, and Aidan disappeared into the long black car so he could ride half a block up the street to the Conch Reef Resort.

The guys who wanted to buy the Wonderland so they could knock it down and bury us in the sand.

And catch more fun in the sun with

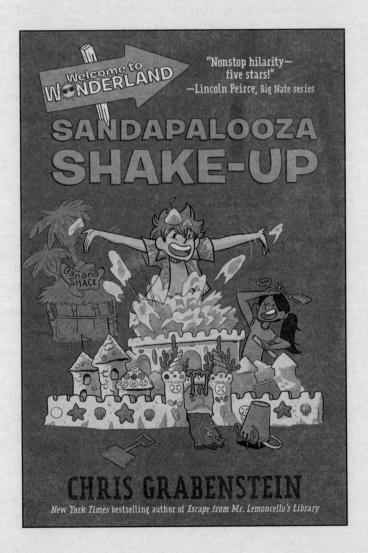

P. T. Wilkie's
Outrageously
Ridiculous
and
Occasionally
Useful
Stuff

How to Say
"Help! The Toilet Is Clogged!"
in Over Twenty Languages!

- Kömək! Tualet tıkanmış! (Azerbaijani)
- Oh, boy. The toilet is plugged up there. (Canadian)
- Jiùmìng! Mǎtǒng dǔ zhùle! (Chinese)
- Pomoć! WC je začepljen! (Croatian)
- Hjælp! Toilettet er tilstoppet! (Danish)
- Tulong! Ang banyo ay barado! (Filipino)
- Aidez-moi! Les toilettes sont bouchées! (French)
- Hilfe! Die Toilette ist verstopft! (German)
- Segítség! Eldugult a vécé! (Hungarian)
- Hjálp! Salerni er stífluð! (Icelandic)
- Aiuto! La toilette è intasata! (Italian)
- Tasukete! Toire ga tsumatte imasu! (Japanese)
- Dowajuseyo! Byeongi ga maghyeoss! (Korean)
- Tuslaach! Ariun tsevriin böglörökhöös baina! (Mongolian)
- Pomóż! WC jest zapchany! (Polish)
- Gargaar! Musqusha waxaa dhaafiyay! (Somali)
- ¡Ayuda! ¡El baño está atascado! (Spanish)
- Msaada! Choo ni clogged! (Swahili)
- Giúp đỡ! Các nhà vệ sinh bị tắc! (Vietnamese)
- Help! Mae'r toiled yn rhwystredig! (Welsh)
- Usizo! Indlu yangasese ivimbekile! (Zulu)

P.T. and Gloria's
Fact or Fiction Quiz:
Florida Edition!

(Circle your answer and find out if you are correct at ChrisGrabenstein.com.)

1. Florida is the southernmost state in the U.S.
FACT or FICTION

2. A crypt in Key West is inscribed I TOLD YOU I WAS SICK.
FACT or FICTION

3. Everglades National Park is home to the slowest-moving river in the world.
FACT or FICTION

4. More people live in New York State than in Florida.
FACT or FICTION

5. Once a year, thousands of Floridians stand at the state line and toss dead fish into Alabama.
FACT or FICTION

6. A museum in Florida is dedicated to shrimp.
FACT or FICTION

7. Florida is the only state that has two rivers with the same name.
FACT or FICTION

8. Gatorade was named after the famous alligator wrestler Ade DePinna.
FACT or FICTION

9. Miami installed the first bank automated teller machine (ATM) especially for Rollerbladers.
FACT or FICTION

10. Venice, Florida, is known as the Shark Fin Capital of the World.
FACT or FICTION

Frozen Green Pond Scum Punch

Ingredients:

- 2 quarts lime sherbet
- 2 liters ginger ale
- gummy worms (or bugs)

Instructions:

- Scoop sherbet into a clear punch bowl. The softer the sherbet, the scummier (and yummier) the punch.
- Add ginger ale.
- Float gummy worms on top.
- Enjoy!

······································

For nonfrozen pond scum (also a tasty treat), try:

Pond Scum Slime Snacks

Ingredients:

- 2 boxes lime Jell-O mix
- gummy worms (or bugs)
- Oreo cookies (optional)

Instructions:

- Prepare Jell-O according to package directions.
- Add gummy worms or bugs (or both!) to clear plastic cups or a glass baking dish. (For a healthier snack, you can substitute cut-up grapes as frog bits!)
- Allow Jell-O to cool partially, and then pour over the worms in the cups.
- Refrigerate until set (two to four hours).
- If you like, add crumbled Oreo cookies for delicious dirt.